MATING SEASON

YAEL MAREE

Mating Season

Editing by: Caitlin Fitzgerald

Cover design: Jennifer Demeter

Interior Formatting: Dawn Lucous, Yours Truly Book Services

This book is dedicated to Cass, Chris, and Catherine.
Without you this would have never existed.

CONTENTS

THE BOOK

The book felt heavy in Ariel's hands. Her face glowed in the firelight as she neared women sitting around the fire. Taking tentative steps on the cooling sand, a hush fell as the young girl approached and tapped her mother lightly on the shoulder. Ariel crouched down to her mother's ear, her eyes fixed on the orange flames ahead.

"Mama Beth? What is marriage?" Ariel's soft voice carried in the dark night as the fire spat and cracked.

"Marriage?" Mama Beth swung back to meet Ariel's eyes, almost spitting the drink from her mouth. "Where did you hear that word, child?"

"In a book."

"A book? It must have escaped the pyre when they burned the rest." Mama Beth gave her a glowering look she didn't understand.

Ariel looked at the older woman with wonder. "What is it?"

Mama Beth took a swig from her whiskey and stared at the girl. "It's just a silly romanticised notion someone came up with a long time ago."

"But what is it?" Ariel persisted.

Her mother sighed and pursed her lips. "The idea was that a man and woman would stay together. Bound for life."

A cackle erupted around the fire from the other women as Ariel frowned, digesting the words.

"But why would anyone want to do that?"

"Precisely, dear. Now, where is this book?"

Ariel fingered the leather-bound book tucked at her side. She had found it that morning. Wedged between the wall and a shelf in the library. Growing tired of her studies she'd explored the stacked racks, scouring the titles while seeking something to distract her.

The red leather peeked from beneath a row of books like a burning sunset beyond the sea. Ariel cleared the shelf digging for the treasure lodged tightly between wood and stone. She clawed at the crisp pages and hardened leather as it bled on the walls, leaving a trail of red marks behind when she finally eased it out of its hiding place.

"Hand it over." Mama Beth's voice was cold.

Ariel's gaze dipped to the book, her fingers tracing the embedded design and golden lettering. Her mother tugged it forcefully from her young arms, and in one fluid motion threw the book into the flames which licked at the pages. They recoiled from the heat, wrinkling and folding in on themselves. One by one they succumbed to the fire which consumed them. With a final puff, the empty spine fell into the pyre, showering the dark sky with tiny golden embers.

Mama Beth turned her back on the girl and resumed her gossiping.

The glow on Ariel's face faded as she retreated from the fire, a sob rising in her throat as she weaved her way back up the path.

Ben sprung out from the bushes. "What did she say?"

"She burnt it." Her lip quivered as she spoke.

"It will be okay, Ariel." He slung his arm around her, barely reaching her neck. At eight she was taller, and he stretched his lanky frame, to comfort her.

"It's fine, I'm fine." She wiped the unshed tears. "Just smoke in my eyes."

CEREMONY

Ariel lay on the beach as the sun-kissed her bronzed body. She gazed at the endless expanse of the sea that surrounded Inan, her island home. The boat would arrive once the sun sets. The thought made her stomach coil. She returned her attention to the sand, allowing it to sift through her fingers. She watched it form shallow mounds on the ever-changing sandbar. The slight breeze toppled the thin structures just as fast as she was building them.

"Heads!" came a shout. Ariel barely registered it, her thoughts on Rosalie's ceremony.

When the ball collided with her cheek, the brutal blow sent pain down to her neck, and her eyes welled in tears. The stinging spread like a flood along her reddening cheek and she stroked the flesh in an attempt to soothe the welt that was already forming.

A light hand fell on her shoulder, and a voice penetrated the pounding in her ear.

"Are you okay?"

Chocolate brown eyes stared at her from behind a mop of sun-kissed hair. "I'm so sorry, Ariel. Are you okay?"

The daze wore off, and she thrust Ben's hand away, the pain giving way to embarrassment when she noticed the group of boys sniggering. "I'm fine, didn't even hurt."

"That was George. I'm going to kill him." Ben's face twisted in a scowl. His chest puffed out, his legs tight ready to pounce.

"Just leave it alone, Ben." She pushed away from him, watching as his body deflated. She rose to her feet. Pivoted in the sand and stormed off towards the village. She ground her teeth as her feet ploughed into the sand. Refusing to brush the agonising pain away.

"Ariel, wait." Ben caught up to her easily, his slender legs slicing through the fine white sand.

"I'm fine, just leave me alone. I have to get home, anyway. Rosalie needs help preparing for tonight."

She continued walking towards the path that would lead her home. Ben followed slightly behind her.

"Your face looks really red…"

Ariel swiveled to face the boy and crossed her arms. "Well, lucky it's not my ceremony night, isn't it?" she hissed at Ben, blood roaring in her ears. Then she turned away and bolted up the path.

"Oh my God, Ariel. What's happened to your face?" her mother shouted from across the room while helping Rosalie out of her dress.

"It's nothing, a stupid accident." Ariel dropped her head and tried to avoid her mother's gaze.

Mama Beth grabbed her daughter's chin with claw-like fingers, the dry, leathery skin digging into her wounded flesh. Mama Beth studied her for another second before nodding slightly and returning to undo Rosalie's dress.

Ariel watched her sister as the fabric fell around her. Her fuller body curved in a way that Ariel's thirteen-year-old body hadn't developed into yet. Ariel looked at her own flat chest then back at her sister. The curve of her thigh, her flat stomach and her swollen bosom. Rosalie smiled at her lovingly.

"Come help me." Rosalie held her hand out to Ariel who took it, happy to get away from her mother's scrutinising eyes.

They slipped into the bathroom where a porcelain bath stood full with steaming water. The floating leaves on the surface gave off a fruity fragrance which hung in the moist air.

Rosalie sunk into the water with a sigh. Her long black hair floated like seaweed on the waves. Ariel grabbed the bucket and filled it with bath water. She let the water cascade over her sister's hair, the black locks sticking to her head. Ariel squeezed the pearlescent lather into her hand and began massaging it into her sister's scalp.

"Are you nervous?" Ariel whispered.

"I am. But don't tell Mom."

"You know I won't."

"I know." Rosalie's dimples deepened as she smiled.

Ariel removed her hands from her sister's scalp and moved over to the side so that she could look at her. "What do you think it's going to feel like?"

"I have no idea. Most of the women said the first time was painful and uncomfortable, but…" she whispered conspiratorially, "they also said it gets better later." She winked. Ariel shrugged, not really understanding what she meant, or how it would be possible.

"Well, maybe it will happen for you the first time around, and you won't have to go a second time…"

"Oh, Ariel, you're so naïve."

"I am not." Ariel scowled and unceremoniously poured hot water over her sister's head.

"And immature." Rosalie laughed, splashing her with a slap of a hand across the water. She then submerged completely into the bath, hiding from her sister's onslaught of water spray. Coming up for air, she was hit with a face full of water. "Stop, Ariel, stop." She held her hand in front of her face. "Mom is going to kill us."

Both girls scanned the bathroom floor, which was now completely flooded.

"I'll clean it later. You better get ready." Ariel gave her sister a hand and yanked her up, helping her out of the water. She watched the droplets slide down her sister's body, forming small rivulets on her curves, before handing her a towel.

"Rosalie, are you going to be okay?"

"Of course, Ariel." Rosalie reached for her sister's hand and placed the other on her bruised cheek. Rosalie crouched down so she could look into her concerned hazel eyes. "This is what men and women do. It is what we are meant for, made for. Don't worry, I'll be fine. I'll tell you all about it when I get back next week."

"Promise?"

"Promise." She snaked her arms around her and pulled her in.

"Now, I better go." Rosalie kissed her lightly on the forehead then left Ariel to mop up the mess.

Ariel sighed and threw the towel on the floor, allowing it to soak the water. The heat was already seeping from the open door, and the sweet fragrance had become overwhelming. Her heart pounded as she squeezed out the fabric. She feared for her sister's safety. She would have to wait a whole week to find out what happened. Ariel wasn't totally naïve, she had an idea of which parts went where, but the whole concept felt foreign and unnatural. If women were meant to be had by men, surely they would all live together. Her thoughts whirled with the dirty bath water, which drained with a slurp, leaving behind only soap scum which Ariel brushed away.

When she joined her mother and sister in the main room, Rosalie was draped in a sheer, almost transparent white dress. A clasp at the back of the neck held the material in place. Made for easy release. Her pink nipples stood firm against the brushing of the fabric, and her lacy underwear fully visible beneath. Rosalie's hair had been dried and brushed, a red flower tucked among the waves.

Her lips, plump and pillowy, glistened with lipstick the colour of pomegranate seeds, and her eyes darkened by the sweep of the black eyeliner.

Ariel gasped. "You look beautiful, Rosalie."

"Thank you." She flashed her a nervous smile.

"Come on, girls, we need to go." Mama Beth feigned nonchalance well, but her whiskey breath and tense jaw did not go unnoticed by Ariel. Mama Beth was never one to show much emotion or affection towards her girls, and today was no exception.

The sisters stepped out onto the porch. The light breeze whispering between the palms carried with it the faint smell of smoke as it rose from the beach. They watched the trail of torchlight as it streamed from the village to the beach like the flow of lava. The night air was hot, and already Ariel felt the sweat pool under her arms.

Mama Beth stumbled out of the house and grabbed the waiting torch. Hay flickered then burst into a hot flame as the air filled with smoke and light. The three made their way to the beach where others had begun to gather.

All the women of the island of Inan congregated along its shores. Gossip and cackling laughter ensued as the entire North Village assembled.

Ariel stepped off the path and onto the beach. The sand,

still warm from the day's sun, shifted under her feet. Firelight bounced off the darkening water as the sun's last rays disappeared beyond the horizon.

A shrill siren wailed across the island, piercing the chatter. The beach fell silent, a nervous energy washing over the women. Only the crackling of burning straw and the lapping of waves remained as hundreds of eyes scanned the endless sea.

A single voice rose from the crowd. "The boat. I can see it."

A solitary light flickered in the distance. It glowed as it advanced ever closer, surging with the gentle sea.

As one, the women moved, their feet firm along the boundary of beach and water. Ariel scrunched her toes, relishing the wet soggy sand beneath as it gave way to her feet. She reached on either side of her and held the offered hands. She had always imagined that if she climbed the highest peak of Inan during a ceremony, she would see the entire island encompassed by women holding hands in a perfect circle.

The women began to hum, a soft sound that washed across the water, welcoming the boat to its shores. Ariel knew three more boats were approaching somewhere in the distance and would soon be docking at the other villages.

Before she could dream about far-off lands, the women began reciting:

> **A mother and father across the sea,**
> **We send them together to welcome thee,**
> **A seed to take root,**
> **come forth new life,**
> **as one heart we long for thee.**

When the women completed their chant, they embraced. Mothers and sisters bade well wishes to those clad in white, as they made their way to the dock where they would board the waiting vessel. Praise and good wishes rang out as they were fare-welled.

Ariel clung to her sister, tears welling in her eyes.

"It will be fine, Ariel. I have to go now." Rosalie's voice shook.

"Let her go, Ariel. You're making a fool of yourself. Don't spoil this for your sister." At the admonition, she released Rosalie and stepped back, her insides quivering.

Mama Beth reached for her eldest and wrapped her arms around her. "Go and come back with my grandbaby." She kissed her on both cheeks and stroked her belly. Then she released her daughter, allowing her to weave her way to the waiting boat.

It was easy for Ariel to spot the debutants. The nervous giggle, the tense jaws, and those who had done it all before. Some excited, some jaded.

The women on shore waved as the boat broke free from the jetty and rocked gently into the black waters. Ariel could just make out her sister's form as the boat drifted farther and farther away. One day she would know where the boat went and what happens on the island of Ishmin. For Mating Season came four times a year, and on her eighteenth year she would find out, whether she wanted to or not.

As the boat disappeared out of sight, many of the women returned to the village while others made campfires on the beach and drank, sharing stories, reliving their youth.

Ariel turned towards the village. The familiar path which cut through the shrubbery like a dense wall against the fierce breeze, was all that stood between the ocean and the simple buildings built into the mountain face. Though she had never left the North Village, she imagined the mountain was peppered with these houses on all sides, creating the four villages of her island. There were no carved paths which connected the four villages, and so, most of Inan had remained a mystery to her.

She was in no mood to face Mama Beth or her own bed. So, she turned her back to the path and walked along the beach, away from the women and the village, her doubts consuming her.

"So, Rosalie left?" Ben's voice came out of the darkness.

Ariel flipped around, her heart pounding her chest. "Shit, Ben, you scared me!" she shouted at the boy standing by her side.

"Sorry, Ariel."

She brushed him off as she continued walking, taking in short, sharp breaths and trying to regain her composure.

"So, Rosalie?" he tried again, murmuring as if afraid to frighten her again.

"Yes, she's gone." Ariel bit her lip, the tears welling once more.

"Are you okay?"

"I think so. I just hope she'll be okay."

"Of course she will."

Ariel fell to the sand, her knees digging into the soft powder. She watched the rhythmic sputter of the waves as Ben shuffled next to her, putting an arm across her shoulders.

"Of course she will," he repeated, "how's your face?"

"Still looks better than yours, that's for sure," she teased, nudging him in the ribs with her elbow.

He winced and fell backwards into the sand in mock agony. Ariel ignored him as he writhed around on the sand then gave up competing for her attention.

"Do you want to go hiking tomorrow? It might take your mind off things."

"Sure, I'll be done with chores by mid-morning."

"Great, me too. I'll come and get you from your house." Ben rose to his feet.

"Sure."

He gave her a wide grin which she missed as she stared fixedly at the dark ocean.

"See you tomorrow," he cried over his shoulder as he ran off towards the village.

3

BEN

"Keep up, slowpoke," Ben teased from the peak. He stretched out a hand and pulled Ariel to the top of the rock where they had a splendid view of the island. Their skin gleamed with sweat.

Ben lay on the hot rock, panting, an arm across his eyes, shielding them from the sun.

Ariel sat on the edge of the cliff, taking deep breaths. "Rosalie is out there somewhere." She stared into the distance where, behind the haze of the sleepy sea, just able to make out a trace of Ishmin Island.

"She is. She'll be back next week." His voice was calm and soothing.

"Do you think…" Ariel paused.

"What?"

"Never mind." Her cheeks flushed red.

"What is it?"

"Do you think it hurts?"

"What?"

"You know… *it*?"

Ben sat up and scrunched his face. "I don't really know. But I don't think humans would have to do *it* if it did." He jumped up and extended his hand. "Come on, let's keep going."

They trekked farther into the thick canopy which shielded them from the blazing sun. The world became a blanket of cool, moist green, and the soft white sand of the beach gave way to a sludgy black mud which squelched under their feet, sliding between their toes. The forest sang with insects and birds as they pushed their way through the shrubbery.

They reached the turquoise water pool in the clearing. Every time she broke through the bush and into the open space, Ariel remembered the first time they encountered the hidden oasis two years earlier.

When they had discovered it, they had ventured into it with great trepidation, inching to the water's edge, inviting and clear. Ariel shrieked as Ben dived into the water, heedless and without a care of what may be hidden within. Seconds passed, and still, he did not emerge. Then a few seconds more. When his head broke the surface, it was with a screech that turned her blood cold. He thrashed and screamed and sent Ariel into a panicked frenzy. She'd yelled his name, helpless from the shore, as he struggled and splashed, the entire pool quivering with his pleas for help. He sank beneath the surface again, and the silence that followed was more petrifying than his cries.

It was then that Ariel noticed it, the water had remained clear. There were no stains on the surface. No remains. The calm water came alive with bubbles, and from beneath Ben broke the water's surface, his expression contorted with laughter.

"You should have seen your face." He slapped the surface as he floated casually on his back. She held back her angry tears, her heart hammering in her chest. His face darkened at her reaction and despite his ongoing apologies, Ariel still wasn't sure if she had forgiven him for the stunt.

"Race you." Ben was already running through the clearing, peeling off his shirt. Ariel didn't bother. She knew if they raced, he would win. On land, Ben always won. She was enjoying the walk, the soft leaves crunching underfoot, the slight breeze that meandered through the trees.

When she reached the water's edge, Ben was floating on his back, showboating. Ariel shook her head in mock disgust and stripped her dress off. Her slight bikini clung to her skinny body, and she padded carefully into the cool water, stopping at hip height to adjust to its cooler temperature.

Ben disappeared beneath the surface then reappeared in front of her, soaking her with a liberal spray of water.

"Ben!" She stood rooted for a second and then leapt and pushed his head under. He reached for her hands and yanked her below. She wiggled free and pushed off his body, diving deeper into the pond. Despite his attempts, once she was free, he could not catch her. Ariel always won in the water. Averting his every attempt at capture, she swam ashore.

He joined her on a patch of flattened grass where she was drying off, beads of water dripping down their hair and skin. They lay quietly, soaking in the sun's rays.

Ben broke the sleepy silence. "Are you going to miss me when I leave?"

"You're not leaving yet."

"No, but I will one day soon."

"Of course, I'll miss you. You're my best friend." She gave him a reassuring grin.

"What if one day I could be more than that?" His eyes focused on her face.

"What are you talking about?"

"Well, you know, one day I'll go to Dagon, and you will stay here, but you will be summoned for the ceremony and maybe we… you know…"

"Oh, gross, don't even think about that." Her heart was suddenly in her throat.

"Why not?" His gaze remained rooted on her face.

"It's just gross. Anyway, I wouldn't want you touching me with your *thing*." She could feel the blood rushing to her cheeks.

"How do you know? Have you even seen one?"

"Yeah." She gave him a sardonic look. "I do work in the nursery, you know. All the boy babies have them. Anyway, you used to pee in front of me all the time when we were little."

"Well, I'm not a baby anymore, am I?"

"You sure act like one half the time." She giggled as he pulled a face.

"Well, do you want to see it or not? I'll show you mine if you show me yours."

Ariel fell quiet, considering his challenge. Her heart thumped in her chest,

Ariel stood on shaky legs and rubbed her forearm. She stared and cocked her head at Ben, daring him to stand up. She licked her dry lips.

When Ben stood up to meet her, she tried to swallow against her constricted throat. "Well, are we doing this or what?" Her voice quivered.

With one hand she reached behind her back and pulled on the slim strap of her bikini top. She slid her free hand under the loose fabric and covered up her chest. Satisfied she would remain hidden under her arm, she slipped the top over her head.

Ben ran a hand through his hair and let out a long breath, the features of his boyish face taut.

Her heart jolted in her chest as she inhaled deeply then allowed her hand to drop, exposing her perky nipples on small swollen mounds that were just budding breasts. She slipped two thumbs into her underwear and stared at him; she wasn't backing down.

"On three," she said, stumbling over the simple words.

Ariel waited for him to slip his hands around the elastic of his pants.

"One…" her voice shook.

"Two…"

She choked as she spluttered out, "three."

Looking just beyond the line of his shoulder, not daring to look elsewhere, she slipped out of her bikini bottoms and stood bare in the forest.

When she took courage to look into his face, she saw Ben, his mouth slightly agape as he feasted on her body with wild, uncertain eyes, his chest heaving as if he had forgotten how to breathe.

A rock had formed in her throat, and she swallowed hard, then unwavering, allowed herself to scan his body, down the familiar flat skinny chest divided by perfect squares along his abdomen, down the narrowing line of his torso until her gaze landed between his legs.

What used to be bare skin was now peppered with black curly hair, his stiffening penis leaning to one side as if deciding if it wanted to be rested or fully erect.

They stood in silence, lingering, each taking in the other.

"I told you I wasn't so small anymore." His chest puffed out, rising and falling in erratic breaths.

"You call that thin worm big?" She smirked as he turned red around the ears.

"Bigger than that flat chest of yours." He covered his mouth as soon as he'd said it, but Ariel was already gathering her bikini, slamming her legs through the bottoms. "No, wait. I was only joking."

"Yeah, well, it wasn't funny." She felt the heat of her cheeks as they burned.

"Ariel, wait." He stepped closer. "I didn't mean anything by it. You are beautiful."

"Well, I did! I don't care what you think! You have a

piddly little worm, and I never want that thing near me again."

She tied the knot of her bikini top behind her back and took off through the forest towards the cliff, her face already burning with tears.

4

HOME COMING

It was easy to avoid Ben. Ariel asked her mother for extra chores and managed to fill her days watching over the newborns in the nursery and helping the expecting mothers in the hospital wing. Ariel was assigned to the nursery at age ten. While her empathetic and caring nature played some part in her placing, her mother being a midwife meant that inevitably, she too, would inherit the knowledge and one day deliver life into the world. Ariel liked the prospect. It seemed like a natural progression. She was delighted to hear that her ninth year would be the last in the fields.

The week without Rosalie went by quickly, and on the seventh day, Ariel finished all her tasks early enough to ensure she could be waiting for her sister on the beach. Mothers gathered in wait, and Ariel watched the dark line of the ocean until she spotted it, a flame in the darkness fluttering in the soft breeze.

Rosalie was coming home.

The warm water lapped at Ariel's feet as she watched the distant flame growing bigger, its orange light spreading across the water.

A quiet hum of anticipation settled on the welcoming

party. As the boat got closer, shrieks and giggles floated across the water. Figures became clearer as the boat floated gently on the waves.

It docked, and one by one, the women disembarked. Some joyous, others subdued. Ariel searched for her sister's familiar face.

"Rosalie," she called out to her when she spotted her, "Rosalie, you're home." Ariel's face broke out into a smile and tension seemed to seep from every muscle.

Rosalie ran into her embrace and kissed her on her head. "Hi, Ariel."

Their mother joined them and pulled the girls apart. "Let me look at you, child." She studied her daughter up and down and slid her arms across her waist. "Come, you must be tired."

"Yes."

They exchanged a knowing look. "Let's get you home, then."

Ariel laced her fingers into her sister's as they walked through the soft sand and up toward the village.

"I've missed you. Are you okay?"

"I'm fine, Ariel. I'm just tired now." Rosalie gave her a wan smile.

They walked the rest of the way in silence.

Their mother led them into the house and made a beeline for the bathroom where Ariel heard the groan of the pipes. Steam and a fruity fragrance filled the air.

She studied her sister, searching for signs of pain or hurt, or change. But she seemed to be the same Rosalie that had left the previous week.

"I'm okay, Ariel. Stop looking so worried." Rosalie frowned.

"I'm not worried, just curious."

"What else is new?" Rosalie giggled softly.

"How long before you know?"

"Know what?"

"If it worked?"

"At least a month, maybe two... Ariel, please stop asking questions, I just want to rest." She seemed to sink into the couch.

"Okay." Ariel sighed, gnawing on her inner lip.

"Your bath is ready," Mama Beth called from the bathroom, her voice indicating that Rosalie had no choice but to come and join her.

Rosalie peeled herself off the couch and entered the bathroom, closing the door behind her.

This was not the reunion Ariel was hoping for. Ariel sighed and shook her head. She would just have to wait to talk to her sister.

She stopped at the bathroom door and glued her ear to the smooth wooden barrier.

"How many?" Her mother's broken voice drifted beyond the wood.

"Enough."

"So, you lost count. That's good."

"Mom!"

"As long as you gave yourself enough chances?"

"Yes." Rosalie sounded exasperated.

"Good."

Ariel stepped away from the door and pondered their conversation. Rosalie seemed fine. Her mother satisfied. Then why did the whole idea make her feel queasy?

I n the week that followed Rosalie's return, Mama Beth kept Ariel busy by adding more chores to her usual weekly list. In her attempt to avoid Ben, she had foolishly given her mother the notion that she wanted less free time and more work time.

Starting in the early mornings and coming home with sunset meant she could not find alone time with Rosalie. She was grateful for the distraction, as the thought of Ben still made her grimace and her stomach coil, but not knowing what her sister had gone through was gnawing at her.

Ariel hoped to corner Rosalie and to satisfy her curiosity. To be sated with detail and subside her fears of the opposite sex. During dinner she hinted at her desire, her heart pounding with her thirst for knowledge.

When Rosalie told her she had other plans after dinner, Ariel gave her a sour look. Rosalie shrugged apologetically and offered to spend time with her on the weekend, winking as she said the words.

Ariel sighed audibly and frowned, knowing she would have to wait two more days for her answers.

She lay in bed, awaiting her sister's return. She listened for the front door and the creaking of the wooden floor as Rosalie crossed the lounge area and made her way to her room.

Ariel waited, giving her sister ample time to settle, then she slunk from her bed.

Ariel tiptoed towards Rosalie's room and stopped. She heard faint moans coming from the other side of the door which stood slightly ajar. She approached and stood in the doorway, watching her sister.

Rosalie had one hand between her legs and another caressing a breast. She moved lightly to the rhythm of her own touch.

Rooted in place, Ariel was unable to unglue her eyes from Rosalie whose eyes were shut and whose body swelled and fell like the rhythmic crash of waves on sand. Hushed moans escaped her clenched mouth and grew more frequent, more frantic. Her breath catching in her throat. Her thighs moved faster, answering to her hand. She stilled, her legs clenched tightly around her fingers, her face contorted in ecstasy, biting her lip. Collapsing on her bed, Rosalie exhaled deeply.

Ariel pivoted and ran to her room, covering her body under the blanket. She shut her eyes, trying to erase the image of her sister, but all she could see was the rise and fall of Rosalie's thighs. The quiver of her lips, her pert nipples as they danced in the dim light.

When she woke the next day, she felt as if she'd not slept at all. The sun had not risen yet, and her room felt stuffy and warm. There was no breeze on the ocean. Ariel skipped her breakfast. Cringing at the thought of running into her sister, she ran straight to the nursery, seeking a safe haven.

When she arrived, Mama Lucy, the caretaker, sent her away.

"You look tired, Ariel. You've been working too hard. There are enough hands here today to manage without you." Mama Lucy gave her a kind smile "Why don't you take the day off."

"I'm fine," Ariel protested.

"I know you are, Ariel. Now go."

"But…"

"And I won't say anything to Mama Beth if you won't." Mama Lucy winked.

At that Ariel's face broke into an appreciative grin and she turned away, taking the steps two at a time while making her way down the beach. She needed a place all to herself somewhere to think.

Ariel walked up the familiar path and veered into the hidden road she and Ben had carved over the years during their exploration. She climbed the rock face and reached the peak, her arms aching with the effort.

Ariel lay on her back, an arm folded across her eyes just as Ben had done on their last meeting. Thoughts of her sister, her moans, plagued her. Her mind drifted to Ben and the forbidden tingle he made her feel.

Ariel slipped her hand into her underwear. And pulled it out immediately. This was not right. What the hell happened to Rosalie on the island?

"Aaarrrggg," she cried out, hitting the rock beneath her with a fist.

"Not happy to see me, then?"

The voice startled her, and she uncovered her eyes to see Ben standing over her.

"How long have you been standing there?" Her eyes bulged as she fought off the urge to run or push him off the cliff.

"Just got here." He gave her a smile, and she studied his face, searching for signs of tell-tale lies. She couldn't find any. Ariel waited for her heart rate to settle into its normal rhythm.

Ariel avoided Ben's gaze as she felt his eyes on her. She curled and uncurled her toes as she studied the view beneath them when Ben cleared his throat.

"I'm sorry." His jaw was locked.

"You've already said that." Her stomach felt like it might drop off the edge of the cliff if he continued.

"I mean it."

"I know."

"So why have you been avoiding me?" He squatted and drew lines into the sand with a stick.

"I haven't. My mom has had more for me to do with Rosalie away...."

"Don't lie to me..." He looked up at her through long lashes.

Ariel didn't respond. They both knew there would be no point in it.

Ben walked over to Ariel and sat beside her, shuffling over so that their legs touched.

"So..." he began not looking at her, "I have been called."

Ariel's body whipped around to meet his face. "What? Already? But you should have at least another year…"

"I know…"

"So why have they called you now?"

"Because I look too much like a man…" His expression was torn as if he was both proud and annoyed by the prospect.

"Well, I beg to differ." Ariel jabbed him in the ribs, yet neither laughed. "You can't go…" she whispered.

"I don't want to go…" He wrapped a hand around her shoulder.

"It's going to be so boring without you. What am I going to do when you're gone?" She leaned her forehead into her knees.

"I don't know, chores? Anyway, you'll probably be an aunt soon, and you'll have to help Rosalie with her baby."

She nodded as silence descended upon them once more.

"I'm going to miss you, Ben." She looked up at his face, meeting his eyes, her chest feeling heavy.

"Not nearly as much as I am going to miss you." He raked a hand through his hair.

"How can you possibly say that?"

"Because it's true. I…" He cleared his throat, "I love you, Ariel." His voice quivered but his eyes held hers.

Her eyes widened as she gasped, trying to settle the sudden surge of butterflies in her stomach. Ben pulled her closer and leaned in, staring into her eyes for a second before closing the distance, then crashing into her mouth, stealing a short, soft peck from her lips.

Ariel sucked in a breath as he pulled away. His face beamed, a smile colouring his face. Ariel brought her fingertips to her mouth, savouring the echo of his lips.

Ben jumped to his feet. "I have to go."

"Right now?" Her heart pounded in her eardrums.

"My ten-minute break is already an hour too long, and Mama Cassy is going to kill me."

"She will," Ariel scoffed, "when do you leave?"

"The day after tomorrow."

Ariel nodded as if in a daze.

"Can I see you tomorrow? Can you meet me by the pool?" Ben was bouncing on the balls of his feet.

"I'll try," she mumbled through fingers as Ben grinned at her and disappeared, descending the rock face with graceful agility.

As she watched his shape descend the cliff face, she struck out her tongue and licked her lips. Her face broke into a toothy smile that she could no longer contain.

Once back on the beach, she dragged her legs and willed them to get her home. The sensation of lightness wouldn't leave her as if she was floating. She needed gravity to pull her back to earth.

When she walked into the house, she saw Rosalie sitting on the couch reading, her fingers tangled in her hair, twirling it about as she stared blankly at the pages.

Rosalie dropped the book and smiled at her sister when she saw her walk in.

Ariel felt the heat rise to her face as she froze in place. Images of Rosalie's twisted face from the night before washed over her, and she mumbled a quick hello and ran to her room.

Ariel sat on her bed, thinking of Ben, when she heard a knock on the door. Rosalie's face peeked in through the crack.

"Are you okay, Ariel?"

"Yeah, I'm fine," she said curtly.

"Don't be angry with me. I haven't been avoiding you. I've just had some things to do, and you've been busy with chores and Mom…"

"It's okay, don't worry about it."

Rosalie pushed the door open further and stepped in "Okay, now I know something is wrong. What is it? Talk to me."

"Ben. He's been called." The mention of his name made her heart flutter and her stomach tighten.

"Oh Ariel." Rosalie sat by her sister, the mattress dipping with the added weight. She took her sister's hand in hers. "I know how much he means to you."

Ariel let her head rest against Rosalie's arm, and she nodded silently.

"When is he leaving?"

"The day after tomorrow." Ariel inhaled sharply as if hoping to swallow the words back up, forcing them to be untrue.

"Does he know how you feel?"

"I don't feel anything for Ben. He's a silly, immature boy."

"Ariel."

"No," she whispered. Her hand clenched Rosalie's.

"You should tell him."

"Why? Then he will leave, and he will be alone."

"But he would know. And when he sees you again…"

"He won't remember me in five years, and anyway," she pushed off her sister, "he won't want someone who looks like me, not when he can have someone who looks like you…"

"Oh, Ariel, you're only thirteen. Your body will change and grow, and you'll become a woman."

"And then what? Tell me what happens on the Island."

"Not what you think…"

"Rosalie." Ariel folded her arms over her chest and turned her back to her sister.

"Can you keep a secret?"

"Of course." Ariel swiveled back toward Rosalie and lowered her voice.

"I fell in love." Rosalie beamed at her younger sister, who gasped.

"Love?" Ariel's eyes grew big.

"Shhh, keep your voice down. Yes."

"How?"

"Girls!" Their mother's sharp voice put an end to their conversation.

The girls looked at one another and rolled their eyes, then they burst into laughter.

"Girls, there is a dinner to prepare. Get yourselves in here and come help." Mama Beth's voice grew louder.

"This weekend, I promise I'll tell you this weekend. And you must tell Ben how you feel before he leaves."

5

GOODBYE

Ben looked at the red door of the house he had come to know almost as his own. He knew how the hinges creaked and how each floorboard sat just slightly outside its comfort zone. He knew that if he was to swing the door open, he would stare at the tattered blue couch that sat along the living room wall, and that to the left would be the small kitchen and round table with four wooden chairs. He knew where Mama Beth kept the pots and pans and where she hid her gummy drops and whiskey.

He knew which bedroom belonged to Ariel and how it smelt, slightly musty with her sweat in the mornings, then airy and fresh in the late afternoon sun that poured in through the window and coloured the room white and yellow. In the evening it would smell fruity like her wet hair and the air would be sweltering in the tiny space.

He knew the house as well as he knew himself and he knew the occupants as if they were his own family.

He watched the door, knowing Mama Beth would step out first, shouting profanities and swearing at the gods as she urged her daughters to hurry their sorry assess. There was always another chore to be done, always a baby to care for, a meal to prepare, clothes to wash, help to give, books to read, medicine to carry.

On his last day on Inan, he didn't want to watch from afar as Ariel would stand and peel potatoes or cut meat or prepare fruit for his final meal. The thought tightened the rock in his stomach, worsening his already sour mood.

The door flew open, and Mama Beth sprawled out, "Come on, you two. We have a lot to do today."

Rosalie and Ariel stepped out behind her, giggling to themselves.

Ben ran up to Ariel and grabbed her by the hand.

"And what do you think you're doing?" Mama Beth's sharp tongue lashed out at the boy.

"Morning, Mama Beth" Ben gave her a weak grin, "I just wanted to speak to Ariel for a minute."

Mama Beth raised an eyebrow and nodded slightly. "Don't take all day about it." Her lip rose slightly at the corner in a sneer, and she walked off, waving for Rosalie to follow.

Ben pulled Ariel by the hand. "Let's go."

Ariel stood, allowing her hand to drop out of his. "What are you doing?"

"Come on."

"Come where?"

"Does it matter? We have just one day left."

"For what?"

Ben shrugged and looked at her blankly. "Just come on, will you? Or do you want to spend our last day together by the door to your house?"

It was their place, and so it was inevitable that they would end up back at their pool. The hot sun shimmered on the turquoise surface. They sat with their feet dangling in the cold water.

"Mama is going to kill me." Ariel sucked in a breath through gritted teeth.

"Probably." Ben smirked. "Lucky for me, I'll be gone, so I'm kind of leaving you high and dry."

"So what else is new?" She gulped down her giggle. "You're always gone when Mama comes to find us." Her lips downturned at the thought. They both knew this time was different.

Ben cleared his throat, changing the subject. "So, have you found my replacement yet?"

"I'm working on it. There are some sweet 11-year-olds that seem up to the task. Maybe, Jacob, he might do," she jibbed.

"He will never be able to keep up with you."

"Maybe not, but he may have to do."

"My replacement doesn't have to be a boy, you know."

"Why? Are you going to be jealous?"

"Like you won't believe." His voice suddenly raspy, his face rigid as an anchor.

Ariel giggled, covering up the lump in her throat.

"Oh, Ben, just stop." She balled her fists, "I can't spend this whole day with you walking on eggshells. We both know what happens tomorrow. We can't pretend that every single thing we say isn't goodbye."

Ben nodded, his eyes flickered from the water to Ariel. He leaned down, resting his body on his elbows, and turned towards her.

"I wasn't joking just now."

"When you said Jacob won't be able to keep up?"

"When I said I'll be jealous."

"Of what?"

"Of every other person that gets to spend a minute with you that I don't." His chest rose and fell in rapid breaths.

"Ben." It was almost a whisper as her heart slammed in her chest.

"I meant what I said the other day, Ariel. I love you." He drew in a long breath, his brown eyes consuming her.

She saw the fear in his eyes as he said it, but Ben was not one to back down because of a little fear. He dared to say and do as he pleased. It had always been part of his charm.

"What could you possibly love about this?" She gestured to herself, her lips pursed, thinking of all the other women on the island and all they would have to offer him.

"You are the smartest, most fun person I know, you never back down from a challenge, fierce like Mama Beth taught you to be. You are kind and compassionate, and you are so beautiful."

Ariel noticed the red blush that had stained his cheeks as he spoke. His vulnerability flooded her veins, making her heart gallop.

With one swift move, he yanked her arm from behind her and caught her head as she fell onto her back, her legs still dangling in the water. Ben rolled himself above her, their faces inches from one another. Ariel stared at him, her pulse skyrocketed, as he swept an errant hair from her cheek.

He leaned his face into hers, their foreheads touching, mingling sweat and skin. They both closed their eyes. The world seemed to have slowed down. All noise had fallen away, and suddenly it was just the two of them. She could feel the warmth of his body as her breathing matched his, their chests falling and rising in unison.

A foreign yet familiar sensation took over her body. A tingle, a spark that only Ben could unleash. She felt it. She knew it was coming. Her entire body screamed for his lips on hers, for his hands on her. She licked her lips and leaned in.

And then the world shattered.

"Ariel, daughter of Elizabeth, Mama Beth is going to kill you!" Rosalie's voice was irate, her red face swollen with effort, her hair wild and sticky, her shirt clinging to her like a second skin as she burst through the shrubbery.

"Oh, sorry." Rosalie's sudden interruption turned apologetic as she took in the scene. She inhaled deeply, calming herself, then looked at her younger sister, whose eyes begun to swell with angry tears.

"Hi, Ben."

He rolled away from Ariel and gave her a wide grin in reply.

"Come on, Ariel. We better go. I think you took it too far today. I have rarely seen Mama so upset."

Ariel frowned, biting her bottom lip, and plucked her feet from the water. She stood up, her hand still in Ben's as he clung on to it. She gave him an apologetic look and jerked her hand away before skulking towards her sister, her shoulders hunched and her face a mask of anger and humiliation.

W hen the sisters arrived home, their mother stood on the porch, a foot tapping furiously on the wooden deck. "Not acceptable, Ariel. I should have known better than to let you run off with that boy."

Ariel said nothing. She knew deep in her heart of hearts that although she had managed to forgive her mother many things, this would not be one. The coal of anger sat in her belly, the ember lit a fire that would burn until her mother's last day.

It was late afternoon, and Ariel's fingers ached with the work. The potatoes had not been peeled for the feast, and although Rosalie had volunteered, Mama Beth insisted it would not be done by anyone other than Ariel. Her fingers grew pruny and sore, the mountain of potatoes seeming endless.

Most of the villagers had assembled at the beach. The tables had been spread and the fires lit. Another ritual, another gathering, but this time there would be no homecoming. When those boys got on the boat they would become men and Ariel didn't know if she would ever see any of them again. Ariel had lost count of the number of times she had had to attend one of these.

Somewhere inside of her, she felt as if it was just not natural. Why were they celebrating loss? That was what it was, each time. She ground her teeth as she continued with her task.

She was still peeling potatoes, knowing no one would be eating them. The music had been coming from the beach for over an hour, which meant by the time she cut all the potatoes and got them cooked, the party would be near over with most of the older ladies drunk and the kids needing a bed.

She threw the peeler across the room. It bounced off the wall with a muted metallic clang. Ariel shot out of her chair. It fell on its back, slamming into the floor leaving a fresh scar in the floorboards.

She began pacing. This was Ben's last night. She had to see him. She would face her mother tomorrow.

Ariel ran to the bathroom. She splashed water on her face, telling herself it was an attempt at washing away the day. She brushed her hair crudely through her fingers and ran for the door.

The cold handle turned, and the door swung open. Ariel froze. Mama Beth sat outside on the porch, a book in one hand, a cigarette in the other.

"Where do you think you are going?"

"To the beach." Ariel's voice quivered.

"Have you finished your chores?"

"You know that I will never get those potatoes done in time." Her voice rose up a pitch.

"Then you shouldn't have run off this morning."

"But's it's Ben! It's his last night." Her throat clenched and tightened.

"And he is a boy." Her voice was clipped.

"What does that have to do with anything? He is my friend. My *best* friend!" Anguish creased her face.

"Because you should learn now, before you get hurt. Don't ever drop everything that needs doing for a man. Get your work done. Get your priorities right."

"What are you talking about?" nostrils flaring as the muscles in her face tightened.

"I am talking about priorities, duties, protecting yourself."

"Protecting myself from what? What are you talking about?"

"One day you will thank me."

"But…"

"No buts. Now get in there and finish your chores."

"I need to say goodbye," she begged.

"Well, if you got your work done this morning, that's what you could have been doing now. Learn this lesson, remember it." Mama Beth's voice was sharp, her tone final.

"I hate you!" Ariel's eyes burned into her mother's shoulder, who turned her back to her daughter and resumed her reading, paying her no more heed.

Ariel swiveled back into the house and slammed the door. Leaning against it, she felt the hot stream of tears as they ran down her cheeks. Ariel straightened. Wiping the wetness from her face, her jaw clenched, she scoured the room, spotting the peeling knife under the couch. Ariel returned to the kitchen and studied the endless pile of unpeeled potatoes as they spilt from containers, coating the entire surface of the table like pebbles of dirt. She raised the knife, lodging it into the starchy unwashed tuber. She raised the knife a second time, bringing it down harder. Chunks of mottled unwashed skin flew across the kitchen as Ariel stabbed at the pile, again and again, butchering the potatoes, until her arm burned with fatigue, and her breaths were but rapid gasps. With a final blow, she wedged the knife into the pile and ran to her room.

She wiped her muddy hands on her sheets as her fists clung fiercely to the fabric. She waited. Silence. Her mother did not follow.

Ariel marched over to her window and swung a leg over the ledge when someone cleared their throat.

She looked down to see Mama Ronda, her mother's best friend, sitting on a chair across from her window. The older woman had brown curls which fell about her face, untamed. The smoke coming from her cigarette smelt harsh and spicy. Ariel sat like a weighing scale, hovering between two sides, in and out.

"You should know Beth better than that, young lady," Ronda tutted, wheezed and took a long drag from the roll-up in her hand. "Better be getting back in there before she comes around." Ronda waved her off as if she was a fly.

Ariel shifted her weight and pulled herself back into her room, slamming the window shut. Her arms fell limply to her sides as her legs crumpled beneath her. She sagged to the floor like a wounded stag, leaning up against the wall. She sobbed into her hands, the muddied tears dripped between her fingers staining her knees. Her shoulders shook as she pressed her head to the hot hard wall.

In the morning Ariel felt an emptiness she knew would never quite be able to refill. She dressed quickly and bolted through the kitchen, bypassing her mother and sister, ignoring the pile of butchered, unpeeled potatoes still waiting for her. Without a word, she flew outside and sprinted towards the beach and down to the jetty.

Families were already gathered by the water. She could hear the distinct cries of women and children. This day was always hard. The tearing apart of families. Mothers letting go of sons, brothers leaving behind siblings. And for Ariel, she was letting go of the love of her life. How could life go on after this day? She wasn't sure, but she dragged herself down to the beach, the white sand sticking to her feet and covering them in a light blanket like makeshift shoes.

She saw him then, his jaw taut his face distraught. He wasn't crying, but she knew him well enough to know he was saving his tears for later. She had seen this face many times before, the mask of bravery. Today he wore it for his mother. He was the last of three brothers, all taken from Mama Cath, all living on different islands, The Shuffling had not been kind to his family, and her children were all far from her. Her home silent. She would bear no more children nor would she ever know her grandkids.

Mama Cath's tears fell hot and fast, landing on Ben's hair, the droplets sparkling in the morning sun. Ariel always wondered why they would send the boys off in these early hours of the morning. Today she knew why. It was so that no trace was left of them by breakfast.

Her body felt heavy under her own weight. She was already mourning his loss, and yet there was his mouth, curving into a beaming smile as he saw her.

He broke from his mother's embrace and ran to Ariel. Their bodies clashed into one another as they held each other. Limbs locked, her face awash with tears, his barely holding on to all he felt inside. His turmoil a perfect picture on his beautiful face.

The blaring siren went off. A final call to board. A final goodbye.

As it wailed, his arms squeezed a fraction tighter around her. Ariel looked at him then, her eyes shone with tears, and she delved into his deep brown eyes. She pushed on her tiptoes, and her lips found his, returning his stolen kiss. Lingering, soft and tender. He tasted like coconut and smelt like the sea. Despite the heaviness in her stomach, it fluttered at the feel of his lips pressed against hers.

"I love you, too," she whispered in his ear as she broke their embrace.

"What are you doing? You must go. Now!" Mama Cath placed a hand on Bens' shoulder.

Ignoring his mother, he pulled Ariel closer still and wrapped his arms around her. In that embrace, the world melted away for a single quiet moment.

Without warning, large arms grabbed Ben's shoulders and yanked at him, he clutched on to Ariel's arms as the foreign hands wrenched him away. He clawed at Ariel, who tried to hold onto him. His nails dug fresh trails along her forearms as he finally let her go.

"Ariel." He screamed for her as the oarsmen lifted him onto the boat, his back hitting the wood with a thud.

Her body sank onto the golden sand below her and suddenly she remembered all the things she had yet to say. All the words she could have said.

"Ariel." His voice carried over the blue water as the two oarsmen pushed away from the jetty.

Though his yells drowned out the crashing waves, Ariel could not look up. Could not meet his face, which she knew would only mirror hers. Her head filled with half-formed regrets. She felt like the sand on the beach, ground to a fine dust, vulnerable to the slightest breeze. Nausea whirled in her empty stomach as she willed herself to look away. She shut her eyes, etching his face into her memories. A hot, painful ember nestled into her stomach, the hot searing pain radiating throughout her body.

"Ariel." Ben's voice grew faint over the water.

She knew she would not be able to make out his face even if she looked and yet still, she could not.

When his voice died away, she searched the horizon, the black speck that was once a boat floated away into memory. She let her tears wash her face as her heart fell into the sand, its broken pieces carried swiftly by the wind.

It was late morning when Rosalie came to find her. Without words, she pulled Ariel up and wiped away her tears with her palm. Lifting her from the sand. Rosalie, acted as her crutch, as Ariel shuffled home.

When they crossed the threshold, Mama Beth remained silent, giving Ariel a look that she didn't understand.

Rosalie helped Ariel to her room and laid her on her bed. Still, her tears fell. Her small body shook as she howled away the pain until she was empty. All that remained was a sobbing mess and then sleep. Beautiful thoughtless sleep.

When she awoke, the house was dark, and her belly was as empty as her heart. She tiptoed to the kitchen and found her mother sitting at the round table, cradling a glass of whiskey. The ice cubes rang out as she took a sip, draining the glass.

"You get one, Ariel. This was it."

Ariel nodded.

Mama Beth stood up, the chair scraping the wooden floor, digging further into the angry white scar that had deepened over the years.

She walked over to her daughter and put a heavy hand on her shoulder. "One day you will understand, and perhaps even thank me." The older woman nodded to herself and shuffled out of the room, leaving Ariel to search for her meal in the fridge.

6

ROSALIE

A soft caress on her cheek woke Ariel. She stretched, taking in a sharp breath and letting it out slowly, as she rubbed her eyes.

"Move over, sleepyhead," Rosalie whispered.

Ariel shuffled to the edge of her bed, allowing Rosalie to slip in beside her. Rosalie lay motionless, allowing Ariel to wake in her own time.

"It's late." Rosalie stroked her sister's arm.

"It's early," Ariel mumbled.

"Depends who you ask."

"It's Saturday, so I don't have to ask anyone." Ariel turned onto her side, her eyes still shut.

Rosalie closed the distance between them and wrapped herself around her younger sister. Her larger body encased the smaller one perfectly.

"How are you holding up, Ariel?"

"Fine, I'm fine." She repeated her usual mantra with a broken voice she hardly recognised as her own.

"Ariel?"

"I'm fine."

"Okay, darling." Rosalie let it go, "It's the weekend."

"I know."

"So…"

"So?" She pulled the sheet over her head.

"So, I told you I'd tell you everything you wanted to know."

At the words, Ariel's eyes shot open and her sleepy body was suddenly alive. She spun around, smashing her elbow into the wall and entangling herself in her sheet.

"Are you okay?"

"Yes, I'm fine. Stop worrying about me and tell me everything." Ariel rubbed her pulsating elbow.

Rosalie giggled. "Almost everything."

"You promised." Ariel pouted.

"I did." Rosalie smiled and buried her head under the sheet.

Ariel joined her. In their quiet white cave, the world seemed safer.

"When we got on the boat I was so nervous, I thought I was going to pass out." Rosalie squeezed Ariel's hand

"But you looked so calm."

"I was a bucket of nerves, and the farther we got from home, the worse it became." Rosalie took a deep breath as if she was reliving the moment. "I sat next to a few girls that had been on Ishmin before and they put me at ease pretty quickly. There was also a bottle of whiskey going around, so that helped." The girls giggled.

"Anyway, we got to the island, and I met the most beautiful man I have ever seen." Rosalie's face broke in a dreamy smile. Her eyes glazed over and she gave her sister a sheepish look.

"What's his name?"

"Chris." She said his name with reverence. "He found me on the first night and we were inseparable. Oh, Ariel, he made me feel so wonderful."

"But you told Mom…"

"I know what I told Mom." Rosalie bit her lip "She doesn't need to know." Her eyes grew wide, imploring.

"Your secret is safe with me," Ariel's face beamed. "Now tell me *how* he made you feel wonderful."

"He told me I was beautiful and I made him feel special. He touched me in the gentlest of ways, and he showed me what love really is."

"Where did he touch you?"

"You know where, Ariel." Rosalie ran a hand down her abdomen and laid it between her legs. "And here too," She pointed to her full bosom and bit her lip.

"Did it hurt?"

"A little at first, but then it was wonderful. You know, a man can make you feel good in more than one way."

Ariel's eyes grew wide at the prospect. Her nose crinkled and her mouth pursed as she thought. "So, you were with no with others?"

"There was no need, not when we love each other. He promised to only mate with me, and to wait for me until I return. And oh, Ariel, I can't wait to go back!" She gave her a lopsided grin, her face flushed with a pink glow.

"I'm so happy for you, Rosalie." Ariel threw her hands around her sister.

"Thank you, Ariel, and one day, maybe, who knows, you and Ben could..."

"Gross, no! He's like my brother." Her face screwed up and she pushed Rosalie's body away.

"Whatever it was you were doing at the pond the other day, it was not something brothers and sisters do." Rosalie smirked.

Ariel felt the heat touch the tip of her ears.

"Sorry I interrupted..."

"Don't, it's fine."

"Ariel."

"It's fine," Ariel said with finality and broke the spell by pulling the blanket back over their heads and exposing them to the sunshine which now poured into the room. "I'm hungry."

Ariel climbed over the body of her big sister and left the room.

7

MIA

The lanky blonde girl was shushing the baby. It had been screaming for almost ten minutes, and she was getting frustrated, unable to soothe him. She tried feeding, burping, dancing, singing and shoving a dummy in his mouth. Nothing worked. Ariel had never seen her before.

"Here, let me." Ariel stretched out her arms and took the crying baby from the girl, who seemed relieved.

Bouncing the baby boy gently against her chest, she had him asleep in a few moments.

"How did you do that?" Large green eyes studied her from above.

"He was just tired. He was giving all the cues. Sometimes they just need a familiar smell."

"They can smell you?"

"Sure. I am here almost every day. My mom is one of the midwives…"

"Oh, wow. So have you ever seen one… you know… come out?"

"Yeah, I have."

"And is it a miracle like everyone says?"

"Mostly it's a miracle no one has murdered my mother during the whole thing, blood, screaming, pain... Kind of makes me get why the men stay on another island."

"Sounds amazing."

"Yup, that's exactly what it is," Ariel said drily, her expression deadpan.

"Mia." The blond girl introduced herself in a fit of laughter.

"Ariel." She smiled back and shook her hand limply. She didn't want another friend. She ached for Ben, and his absence gnawed at her. Her wound raw, even after a year-and-a-half of absence. No one could replace the chasm he had left so empty. Ariel wanted to hate Mia, but her genuine smile and kind face drew her closer.

"I've never seen you before."

"Yeah, we arrived with the boats last week. Our family was chosen for The Shuffling, so here we are."

"Oh." Ariel's eyes fell to the sleeping baby.

"It's okay. It was a small island, anyway, and it's always just been my mom and me. My brother was chosen for The Silent Army years ago." Mia winced then shrugged, brushing it off. "Seems like there's so much more to do here. Maybe you could show me around later?"

"Maybe I could." Ariel smiled and put the sleeping baby in his cot. A lull fell on the nursery as the babies slept peacefully. "So, a chosen guard and a shuffle, your family's number must come up a lot."

"I guess so, but the elders know what they are doing."

"Do they?"

"Of course they do. Otherwise we would all be walking around with two heads and six toes."

"Right..." Ariel took a step back.

"Anyway, aren't you worried about being shuffled?"

"Us?" She almost laughed at the prospect. "Mama Beth

would never allow it. She is an institution here. I'm stuck here forever." Her shoulders slumped as she said the last.

"That might not be the worst thing." Mia nudged her.

"How can you be so sure? You've only been here for five minutes. I've been stuck on Inan my whole life."

"And I'll never see Junodei again." Mia's smile faltered" It will always be my home."

"Is this your job?" Mia whispered, not allowing the unease to settle.

"Yes, turns out I'm pretty good with babies."

"You sure are," Mia agreed, nodding at the shorter girl.

"My sister is pregnant again. She is due in a few months." Ariel beamed.

"That's amazing."

"It sure is."

"And will you be at the delivery?'

"I don't think I will have a choice."

"That's okay." She grinned at Ariel. "One day she will be at yours."

Ariel grimaced and nodded. She walked over to one of the cots and patted a sleeping baby, hoping to bring the topic to a close.

When the shift was over and the new crew had been briefed, Ariel bid Mia farewell and wished her a good afternoon.

"Really? You're going to ditch the new girl just like that? I may not even know how to find my way home. You will come here tomorrow to find my frozen, starved body on the steps of the nursery. And the babies will be scarred for life."

Ariel couldn't help but laugh at the melodrama exuded by the strange new girl.

"As if?" Ariel put her hands on her hips, "it never gets cold, and there's plenty of baby milk inside the fridge to sustain four grown humans for three weeks. What might kill you are the wet-nurses who pumped all that milk... but you look big enough to defend yourself against a crazed horde of hormonal women…"

Both girls burst out laughing at the image. Ariel clung to her side as her laughter grew.

When they had settled, Mia pouted, "Pretty please?" She cocked her head and fluttered her eyelids.

Aerial exaggerated a sigh. "Come on, then, before I change my mind and let you starve." The girls giggled as they walked off.

Ariel led the way down the dirt road, which had been carved into the mountainside. She pointed at the large building jutting from the bottom of the hill. The white bricks contrasted with the thatched roof.

"That's the kitchen and mess hall."

"Why is it so close to the beach?"

"People love a good view with their dinner," Ariel said drily, chewing on her lower lip.

"Really?"

"Well, there is that, and the fact that we have so many ceremonies. With having to cook so many big feasts so often and cart down to the beach, I guess it was the logical place to have it."

Mia nodded as Ariel went on, "Anyway, the kitchen ladies cook for everyone every night, so you are free to stay and eat at the hall or take your meals home. Many of the childless eat there every night."

Ariel stared at the building, her eyes prickling with tears as she thought of Mama Cath joining her childless ghosts. When she was younger, she would often stay and eat with Ben's family, but after the age of nine, her mother insisted she come home. As always, she obeyed.

She shook her head and turned away from the kitchen. "Maybe it's more fun being alone with people."

Ariel trudged up the path, Mia following behind. They walked by the hospital where – Ariel explained - most often than not, the cold, white structure was the first and last the women of Ishmin saw. Disease was rare, and often, if treated early enough, non-fatal. Those who were deemed too sick to recover would be quarantined, and once deceased, would be burned. One door for life, the other for death.

It was also the only building that was built entirely from bricks salvaged after the great Flooding that sank the world. It was powered by two generators that were used only when necessary. The rest of the time, fire was the only source of heat and light, as it was across the rest of the island.

Ariel pointed out the school, the library and the seamstress building, all wooden and thatched, like most of the homes on Inan. Women were milling about, some with a herd of children following.

By the time they were done with the tour, the girls found themselves walking along the beach. The pair fell into an easy conversation. Mia told Ariel about the island of Junodei. How they had winter where she came from, and how because of it, Mating Season only happened twice a year for them. She discussed their chores and how their island set-up was similar to this one. She loved the fact she could have a swim all year long and was delighted to let her pale white skin be tickled by the sun. Over time she would learn that her skin would never turn the beautiful bronze that Ariel's would, but rather would burn a shade of cherry red and then fade back to paleness.

Ariel always knew someone would come. She knew there would be a day when Ben would be replaced by another. That her friendship would have to evolve and move on, but she wasn't ready for it yet. She wasn't ready for that hole to be filled, and she was angry and delighted. She was angry at herself for allowing Mia to fall so quickly into the void. Yet she felt relief, because if that hole would've been allowed to stand empty for much longer, she would have fallen into it herself, maybe unable to crawl out even if she tried.

Despite putting up some resistance, Ariel found herself opening up about Ben.

In time, the void shrank and filled with Mia's loud personality and wholehearted laughter. Ben's memory grew softer, like a dream that clung on after wakefulness.

8

EIGHTEEN

On her eighteenth birthday, Ariel woke up wanting to cry. Her stomach churned at the thought of getting out of bed. She knew that today was the day that everything was going to change, whether she liked it or not.

There would be a party at sunset. All the girls who had come of age would be celebrated. There would be dancing and drinking and feasting. But it was not tonight she was worried about. It was the following day. Then she would be examined like one of the animals in the stables. Her mother would poke and prod her. The internal working of her body would be scrutinised in the most intimate and uncomfortable way possible and then she would be dated and set. After that, she didn't want to think about what came after.

Her ceremony.

She doubled over, the knot in her stomach tightening. She wasn't ready. She had never been ready, and no matter what anybody told her, that wasn't going to change just because of her age.

Her mother's voice pierced the silent house. "Are you up yet? Jobs need to be done, just because we celebrate tonight doesn't mean you get to be lazy today, too."

"Yes, yes I'm up, I'm coming," Ariel yelled from her bed then pushed her body up from her mattress, forcing herself to get up and get dressed. Bile sat in her throat, threatening to erupt. She joined her mother and Rosalie in the kitchen where she found the older woman with tears in her eyes, her arms wide open and a proud look on her face.

"Oh, my darling Ariel, my baby girl. Today you are a true woman, and I'm so excited for you! Soon you're going to go on a journey where you will fulfill your true purpose and your duty to our civilisation." Her mother's face glowed with joy as if she was reliving her own journey as she spoke.

"We are soon going to have more children in this house. I can't tell you how excited I am. Pity your sister didn't carry on mating. Look at her; she is a breeding machine. She could have easily mated another two or three times." She pursed her lips, looking at Rosalie who paid her no heed. "But never mind that now. We have you to bring home strong babies."

"I don't want to talk about that, Mum." Ariel wrapped her hands around her waist, fighting the nausea.

Mama Beth's voice took on a sharper tone as she said, "Enough with your nonsense, Ariel. Let's just enjoy this day, please."

Ariel nodded and sat down, her breakfast already cold. As she took her first mouthful of cold eggs, she thought of Ben. It had been years since she had allowed herself to think of him, but if she was celebrating her birthday, he was sure to be celebrating his.

A sudden flush filled her cheeks as she wondered if he might be at Ishmin or if he had been taken by The Shuffling. Chewing the inside of her lip, the thought was both delighting and daunting. The egg felt like paper in her mouth. She grimaced and spat it out, what little appetite she had vanished with the prospect of running into Ben, or never seeing him again. She pushed away from the table and dragged herself from the house, her legs threatening to collapse with each step.

The day was just like any other. Ariel spent the morning in the nursery, with Mia clucking about her like a concerned mother hen. Despite her efforts to thwart her off, Mia kept asking about her mood and wellbeing. Ariel was happy to see the shift end and left Mia talking to Mama Lucy, finally making her escape.

She knew that in the evening there would be a great celebration for the new generation of vessels, and that she was one of those vessels. She hated the name; she hated that idea. All she wanted was to be free of the burden.

After her evening bath, her mother brushed her long hair. The sensation a combination of melancholy and dreams. When she was but four or five, Mama Beth would brush her hair before bed. It was a lovely time to spend together in serenity.

"Tomorrow you will begin preparations for your ceremony." She stroked Ariel's face with her fingers as if releasing her baby into the world. "You are so beautiful, Ariel. You will have beautiful children, just like your sister."

Mama Beth shot Rosalie a quick glance. The once beautiful woman a wilted flower. Her long black hair unkempt, her full figure shapeless. Her flawless skin a scarred oasis.

Ariel lowered her eyes, unable to look at the sister she loved so much. Her heart broke a little more each time she held her two nephews, knowing that in a short few years they would all have to say goodbye, maybe for a lifetime. She saw how the ache of that future was eating at her sister. No words that could be said would take her out of the lull of sadness that now shrouded her. Rosalie insisted that one day the future would become the present. She couldn't enjoy her boys now. She may never enjoy them, not if she had to lose them one day, just as she had lost Chris.

"Have you not shed enough tears over men, Rosalie? You are giving your sister the wrong idea. You always had, ever since you got off that damn boat that last time." Mama Beth huffed, "No need to cry over spilt milk; it is the way of the world."

"But why does it have to be?" Ariel pushed away from her mother.

"Not tonight, Ariel."

"But why?"

"Hush, child. Go and make sure the boys are sleeping. There is much to talk about."

When Rosalie could no longer take care of the boys, Mama Beth asked her to return to the house. Mama Beth looked after the boys in a manner much different to that of her own daughters. Soft embraces and stroking of hair, no stern words or admonitions about being dirty or making a mess. Ariel hurried to her sister's room where the boys were asleep, huddled in their beds. The two were inseparable, just as Ariel and Rosalie once were.

When she returned to the main living area, the room was illuminated only by the small flickering flames burning on the ends of three candles Mama Beth had placed on the floor. She sat cross-legged in front of the burning wick, her face awash in yellow and orange light. Without a word, she gestured to her two daughters to take position in front of the remaining candles. Rosalie wrenched herself from the couch with a groan and lumbered over, sinking to the floor, the flame flickering wildly before her. Ariel was the last to complete the circle as she sat and watched the quivering light dance about the room.

"Ariel, daughter of Elizabeth, tomorrow you will attend your first ceremony, and you will go forth to do your duty. You, pure of heart and soul, will go to find yourself a mate, one who is worthy of your smile, of your charms and of your body. You, sweet child, have all the power. You will choose your own path, and you will have the power to say yes or no."

Mama Beth paused, allowing the words to sink in, the same words which would be spoken in many rooms tonight, and that had been spoken for generations. Their longevity gave them power.

"Tomorrow you will set foot on Ishmin, and there you will give yourself to a worthy man with which you will bear children. You will give your body to him fully and without hesitation, and you will enjoy his delight in you. And when you return, if you have been blessed with a child, you will have fulfilled your duty to our people."

Mama Beth's eyes gleamed and glowed in the candlelight.

"Tomorrow at the birth of night you will be birthed a new person, a woman, no longer a girl. The swell of the sea will wash from you your youth and will lead you to womanhood as you sail toward your mate. Be sure to use your wit and prowess to pick the perfect alpha male."

"How would I know?"

"You will know."

"There are rules on Ishmin, as there are on Inan, and these you must remember." Her mother's face looked stern as she passed the rules on to her daughter.

"The Watchers observe; they see and hear everything. You must obey their law on their island, for you are their guest. No man can strike a woman nor force himself on her in any way. No woman could do the same. No man can proceed with the mating unless the woman has agreed wholeheartedly. All occupants of the island must choose at least one mate before their seventh day, or one deemed suitable for them will be chosen by The Watchers. Copulating with the chosen mate is not looked upon as forceful. It is part of the law for the Takers to take. All guests can mate with numerous partners, and it is in fact encouraged that you do so to increase the chances of insemination – all mates must be recorded by the seventh day to ensure no inbreeding. Watchers will intercept if inbreeding is suspected."

"Do you have any questions?"

"Will it hurt?" Ariel looked to her sister, her chest constricting.

"Maybe a little, just the first time," Mama Beth answered in her stead.

"What if I am not ready?" She wrung her wrist, the taste bile in her throat fresh once more.

"There is no such thing. Your body is at its prime to bear children, and so it should."

"But what if I am not ready?"

"Then prepare yourself to be ready. You've had an entire lifetime to prepare for this day."

"But what if I am not?" Ariel stood up and paced the room, the nausea building in the pit of her stomach.

"Then drink or close your eyes. Either way, sweet child, this is your duty."

"But I am more than just a vessel, more than just a body." She swatted the air.

"No, Ariel, you are not!" Mama Beth's voice held a sharp and dangerous edge as she hissed the words.

"But you said we have a choice." Ariel's voice rose in pitch as she stared down her mother.

"You can choose a mate, you can choose to reject a mate."

"Not if we are taken."

"Don't let it get to that!" She slammed her hand on the floor. "You are no longer a child. Stop acting like one! You're just like…" Mama Beth muttered something to herself swallowing the rest of the sentence.

"Like what?" Ariel's blazing eyes lingered on her mother.

"Hush now, let's celebrate."

With that, her mother produced the bottle of whiskey

which had been tucked behind her. The clinking of the shot glasses rang in the silent room. She poured the amber liquid and handed one glass to Rosalie, who was still sitting meekly on the floor. She took the other and stretched out her arm, forcing Ariel to walk over and accept it. "To cleanse the soul and your pipes." She raised her own glass and hissed as she tossed the alcohol into her throat. Mama Beth poured herself another. "This one is to oil my bones."

Ariel scrunched her face as the bitter taste of whiskey stung her tongue and burned a warm trail down her throat.

"Tomorrow morning, we will begin your cleansing. We shall soon go and celebrate your coming of age, and then you must ensure to get some rest, because if my memory serves me right," she grinned and winked at her daughters, "you are going to need it." The older woman chuckled to herself and disappeared into the back of the house, her bottle of whiskey in tow.

Rosalie returned to the couch. She held her arms open to Ariel, who fell into her, and allowed her to gather her warmth about her.

"Will you come with me tomorrow?"

"You know I won't go back, Ariel." She looked vacantly through the window as moonlight drifted across the floor.

"But maybe you can see Chris again..."

"Ariel..."

"Maybe you can fix it... Try for a girl? You guys can..."

"Ariel! Just drop it, please." Her eyes glistened with unshed tears.

"Okay." Ariel bit her tongue. "I'm scared."

"Why?"

"You know why."

"It doesn't hurt after the first time. I've told you already..." Rosalie sounded exasperated.

"That's not it."

"Well, maybe you will be blessed with only girls."

"That's not it, either."

Rosalie scrunched her face as if searching for a lost piece of information she knew she had. Her face relaxed as she spoke. "Ben? Are you afraid he won't be there? Or that maybe he will be?"

"I haven't thought about Ben in years." Ariel's voice sounded foreign even to her.

"Sure, you haven't." Rosalie smiled for the first time in weeks, and Ariel found a glimpse of her beautiful sister, the one she used to have.

"And what if he is there? He probably hasn't thought about me in years. Anyway, it's Ben. That's gross. He's just like our brother."

"But he isn't our brother."

"I know, but – "

"No buts. If you are scared and need a friend, you'll have one. And if you need a mate, I am sure he would be more than happy to do that too."

Ariel jabbed her sister with an elbow. "I'll never mate with Ben."

"But you could."

"No, I couldn't." Ariel looked into Rosalie's eyes and knew she understood.

The girls sat in silence a little longer, knowing that after tomorrow they would once again be different people.

"Come on. you two. A party awaits our vessel." Mama Beth burst into the room. She swung the front door open and disappeared down the path, her bottle of whiskey her only companion.

The moonlight splashed down its silvery light, and they navigated the rough path to the beach by the shadows it cast. The sky was speckled in stars, the humid air clung thick to their skins. As they broke through the curtain of protective shrubbery, they were greeted with the celebrants already gathered at the beach.

Flickering firelight danced across the water, painting the inky black a shimmering orange. Bonfires were lit across the hundred-mile stretch of beach. Tables laden with party food lined the seashore, each stacked with fruit, cakes and alcohol.

The beach was littered with all of Inan's inhabitants. Children and women were rejoicing in the coming of age of a new generation's passing. Tonight would be a celebration and tomorrow would be a rite of passage. The older women who no longer bred would pass on the torch to this new generation of vessels who would bring forth more children and keep the species alive.

Although pestered by Mia, Rosalie and her mother, Ariel escaped the first moment she could. She didn't want fire-works and jubilation. She wanted this day to pass quietly in the night, unseen, undetected.

Ariel woke in the late morning light as it streamed under her door. She rolled in her bed, wondering why her mother didn't wake her for chores. The pit of her stomach collapsed, and she was filled with dread as she remembered what day it was. Knowing she could not halt the ebb of time, she fought the urge to vomit. She pushed herself off the bed and stepped out of her room.

"There she is." Her mother smiled at her through a mask of pain. Ariel wondered how much she had had to drink as she embraced the older woman, sour alcohol fumes escaping her like steam.

"Look at what's arrived." Mama Beth pointed to the crisp white dress that lay across the couch. Like a ghost looking for a body to possess.

Ariel returned a weak smile, trying to keep her stomach from erupting.

"Come sit and eat. You will need your strength for tonight." Her mother's eyebrows shot up and down in a dance above her eyes.

"Oh, just stop, will you?" Ariel erupted at the gesture.

"No! You need to stop! I've had just about enough of your attitude. Now, this day is jubilant and not just about you, so stop ruining it with your sour moods and misguided foolery. For god sakes, it's sex, not a whipping." As she walked away, she mumbled to herself, "Although some enjoy both."

Ariel stared at the plate. Bacon, eggs and toast smirked back, daring her to eat them, the usually appealing smell nauseating. She scraped the food into the bin, watching the yellow yolk ooze and sink out of sight.

Ariel splashed water on her face, her hands shaking as she studied her reflection in the mirror. Her mouth formed a rigid grimace as she twisted her hair in a wild bun and left the house toward the hospital.

Ariel sat in the white corridor, the orange plastic chair sticking to her moist skin. Hushed murmurs of conversation filled the narrow space as other newly celebrated vessels filled the row along the wall. The smell of sweat masked the sharpness of the disinfectant. Ariel shifted in her chair, the back of her thigh covered in moisture.

The door creaked open and a celebrant walked out, Mama Kate, the midwife, on her heels.

"Ariel, daughter of Elizabeth."

Ariel unglued herself from the chair and dropped her arms which had been folded around her waist. Her nails left round half-moons in her flesh.

She stepped into the room, Mama Kate shutting the door behind her.

"That is Mama Heidi. She will help with today's examination."

The blonde woman gave Ariel a kind smile and returned to her notes, not getting off her chair.

"Remove your clothes and lay on the bed, please."

Ariel felt her pulse pounding in her temples while undoing the button to her shorts. Her hope slipped away with each layer of clothing that fell to the floor. She concentrated on the spluttering and grunting of the tired generator, powering the hospital wing, allowing for the flow of cool air which covered her flesh with goosebumps and fueling the fluorescent light above, which gave the room an insipid hue.

She slogged to the bed which kissed the wall, her legs heavy. Ariel lay down on the sticky plastic sheet. One hand rested over her bosom while the other covered her pubic region, her legs firmly clamped.

Mama Kate approached her wearing the cold distant look of a doctor at work. "Bring your heels towards your bottom and then let your knees fall to the sides."

Ariel looked to the white empty wall as she obeyed the midwife. She concentrated on the clatter of the groaning machine, imagining she was standing right by it. The rusted red paint peeling off the dented right side sunk into overgrown grass. The stench of old fuel, scarce and precious, bought from the First Quarter. Ariel had often wondered the price.

"Try to relax," Mama Kate added as cold hands made their way inside her. Ariel groaned and bit her lip, her ears burning as the midwife rattled off a series of conclusions to Mama Heidi, who recorded everything with meticulous handwriting.

The hand moved up her abdomen.

"Hands above your head, please." Ariel willed her hands to move as the doctor's smooth fingers palpated her breasts one at a time.

"You're all done, Ariel. Please get dressed." The glove twanged as she snapped it off her hand.

Ariel sat, the plastic sheet sticking to her back. She tore it from her skin like a flayed fish and dressed without a word.

Mama Kate ushered her to the door and held it open. "Thank you."

Ariel didn't hear the next name that was called as she bolted down the corridor and burst outside, gasping for air.

When she returned home, she heard the pipes as they groaned. Water ran as her mother busied herself in the bathroom. Fragrant soap and spices filled the air. When the pipes settled, her mother's head peeked from beyond the wall.

"Take her. She needs to wash."

Rosalie took Ariel by the hand and led her to the bathroom. "You're shaking."

Rosalie helped Ariel undress. It wasn't for lack of trying to do it herself, but she found herself unable to move. Every muscle in her body tensed.

Ariel flinched as her sister pulled her thin singlet from her body and held her as she stripped off her underwear. Rosalie steadied her sister as she slipped into the bath then sat by her side.

"You need to calm down. You're looking a bit green."

"I don't know how…I don't know if I can do this."

Rosalie sighed and studied her little sister. Although they had two different fathers, their mother was once, and still, a beautiful woman, and they had both inherited much of her looks.

"I can help you relax," Rosalie considered her words, "but you must promise not to get embarrassed."

At that Ariel's face lit up. "I won't, just help me."

"Ariel," her sister started, shifting and clearing her throat. "Have you ever touched yourself? You know, down there?"

Ariel's eyes grew incredulous.

"Just listen." Rosalie's voice became firmer. "You keep saying you are afraid, but there are some amazing things our bodies can do. One day you will see that when a man does them for you, they could be even better." She shifted again. "Just try for yourself. Once you do, you will see that you have nothing to fear and you will be much more relaxed."

Ariel stared at her sister through narrowed crinkled slits.

Ever so gently, Rosalie took her sister's hand and guided it between her legs. "Trust me." She gave her a small kiss on the forehead and stepped outside.

Ariel knew she had become a woman but had never given the prospect much thought. Her once flat chest had developed and become swollen and full, her hips rounded and pubic hair covered her sex. She was yet to explore her own body, always pushing away the idea of sexuality. For sex was a thing to be done only with a mate and desires were a thing of dreams.

She let her fingers slip between her legs following her sister's brief instruction. A brilliant memory of Rosalie on her bed those many years ago flashed in her mind's eyes. As her fingers played their beautiful tune, she could feel her entire body come alight. Her pert nipples hardened, the cooler air beyond the hot water kissing them lightly. Her body quivered in delight, the intensity grew, peaking, till she rose through the air floating weightlessly back into the water. She rested. Her body surged, awakened. Her mind clear.

"You look better." Rosalie's mouth curved at the corners.

Ariel snatched the towel from Rosalie, her cheeks burning. With the constant knot in her belly momentarily sated, she stepped into the living area, allowing her mother to dry her hair and dress her in her lacy undergarment and see-through white dress. She heard the clasp as it came to a final resting place behind her neck.

Her mother kissed both her cheeks which were red from heat and delight. Ariel sank into the chair as if it was made of air. She closed her eyes, allowing her mother to lather her face with makeup and seal her mouth with ruby red lipstick.

She styled her hair and tucked a flower in the back just as she had done for Rosalie five years before.

Rosalie looked at her sister, no longer a girl. "You look amazing, Ariel."

Arie gave her sister a shy smile, lacing her hand through hers, and allowed her to lead them to the door.

9

CEREMONY

Ariel's toes clenched and unclenched, gathering sea sand beneath them then releasing it back into the waves. Despite the cool breeze, a droplet of sweat ran down her brow, slicing her cheek. She bit her lip trying to steady herself.

Her light white toga clung to her body, the tips heavy with moisture.

> **A mother and father across the sea,**
> **We send them together to welcome thee,**
> **A seed to take root,**
> **Come forth new life,**
> **As one heart we long for thee.**

The words echoed around her as the wind carried the words over the ocean. She mumbled with the rest yet could produce no coherent words.

She tugged at her dress watching the boat dock. Was it normal to feel like this? She wondered if she would see him. Her heart fluttered at the thought of his name. Would he remember her? Would he want her? Would she know what he looked like?

Arms around her shoulders brought her out of her daze. Rosalie's face looked down on her reassuringly. "You'll be fine. Take your time. Remember the power is all in your hands." She kissed her lightly on the forehead and released her.

Mama Beth pulled Ariel to her and whispered in her ear, "No foolishness, Ariel. You know what's at stake." She pulled away and their eyes met. Mama Beth's eyes flashed with anguish. She steered Ariel towards the boat, which was already filling up with women.

Cold sweat glistened on her furrowed brow as Ariel climbed onto the broad wooden boat. The wet planks felt coarse under her feet. She found Mia already seated on a bench, and she joined her, the smell of fish wafting from the hull.

Fire blazed from the torch attached to the bow. It rose against the dark sky, a plume of grey smoke trailing into the blackness. The heat warmed Ariel's face and coloured the vessels' faces in orange and gold, eyes reflecting in the flickering flames. Ariel studied these faces, some painted with fear and anxiety, others with wonder. The rest, excited and giddy as they held a secret the rest of the women didn't know. Wringing her hands, her body rocked gently with the boat as the final passenger embarked.

The two oarsmen, whose weathered faces seemed tired and bored, climbed back on the boat, pulling the ramp up behind them. Taking their positions, they used their long oars to push away from the sandbank. Within minutes, the faces on the beach became less distinguishable, and the shapes became nothing but black things. The flames of torches flickered like fairy lights as they grew smaller and dimmer in the distance.

Ariel felt Mia's hand entwine into hers. She unglued her eyes from the black sea and looked into her friend's excited face. Her large eyes shone, a faint curve to her lips the top row of teeth just visible beyond her ruby red lips.

"How are you holding up?" Mia squeezed Ariel's hand.

"I don't know, I think I'm okay."

"You look like shit."

"Wow, thanks. Guess I am bound to find a mate then, aren't I?"

"You don't want to find a mate, Ariel. You want to find Ben."

Ariel's body sank as she seemed to deflate. She waved her friend off. "I haven't thought of him in years. Can we just move on from him?"

"Sure thing." Mia raised an eyebrow, her sarcasm laid thick. "Look, we are almost there."

Ariel turned her face back to the water and followed her friend's finger. In the closing distance she spotted Ishmin, outlined by a fierce glow, as if the earth itself was on fire. The waves lapped at the boat, rocking it in a sweet lullaby. A bottle of whiskey got passed around, the whispered conversation growing bolder and louder.

As their boat closed the distance, Ariel noticed the row of torches erected along the beach like a landing strip inviting the boat to dock on its shores. Sparks erupted into the air as the hay burned, embers floated down to the black sea.

The waves pushed the boat closer to the island, and soon the old men jumped from the wooden structure, their legs swallowed by the black sea. Their strong upper bodies pushed it along the sandbank, docking with a long wooden pier that led onto the beach. Ariel's heart thumped in her ears as wood scraped against wood, sending a shudder through the entire structure.

She dismounted, her hands laced in Mia's. The girls

huddled as they took small, tentative steps along the rickety pier, which swayed softly with the song of the waves beneath. Ariel heard faint drum beats. She hoped they were loud enough to conceal the thumping of her own heart.

10

NIGHT ONE

The gaggle of women swayed toward the beach. Their bodies tilted as the jetty tethered then tottered. The woody fragrance of smoke greeted them as they approached the lit-up beach. Ariel took in her new surroundings.

Tents of different colours and size lined the beach.

Her feet landed on sand and she approached the sorting table. Behind the square, foldable table sat an older woman. Her long, white hair framed focused eyes, whose glare travelled with unnerving thoroughness, taking in Ariel's body. She smacked thin lips together as she asked for Ariel's name and age, recording every detail in a long but narrow notebook filled with columns.

Ariel had heard her mother speak of them. The Keepsakes, she had called them. In them, The Watchers kept track of the bloodlines. There would be no mixing of families or generations. It was also how they decided The Shuffling.

The old woman wrote in curved thin lines, her skinny hand dragging slowly across the page, as her skin flailed on her bones.

"Ariel daughter of Elizabeth," the old woman's voice was

kind, "You will be sleeping in the Left Blue tent number Twenty-six."

"Left? Blue? Twenty-six?"

"Yes dear, and do not forget to come register your mates each morning." She gave her a look that indicated Ariel's time was up.

Ariel gave The Watcher a wan smile as she willed her legs to move. She stepped away from the table and toward the makeshift tent city. She took a left to the woman's camp where she wandered among the coloured tents, seeking her accommodation for the next week. The experienced women, those who had borne children and were over the age of thirty were housed in red tents. The younger ones who were between the ages of twenty-five and thirty were taken to green tents. Women under twenty-four were ushered to the blue tents.

Ariel located her tent and stepped inside, her throat closing even as she tried to swallow. She wondered what had become of Mia. They were separated at the sorting. She took another step inside the blue cavern. Four cots were set along the walls, slightly elevated from the sand. She fell on the first one, stashing her small bag underneath. She waited, listening to laughter and chatter as it swept through her fabric walls. Anticipation hung in the air carried, by perfume and smoke.

She kept waiting, yet no one else entered her tent. The emptiness gnawed at her, fraught with all her unanswered questions.

A silence seemed to have fallen over the camp as a siren rose. Like a whistle, it started low then grew in prowess until it drowned out all other sounds. When it had died down, the newcomers, like ants, begun to make their way to their first gathering. The invitation was not to be ignored.

Ariel followed the crowd as they walked along the beach. Her stomach full of led, each foot heavy as if set in concrete, she willed herself to keep up.

The dim drums that had welcomed them to Ishmin now rose in a thunderous beat, the tempo wild and exciting.

As she rounded the dune, an open plain greeted Ariel. Polished wooden planks that gleamed against torchlight covered the levelled sand bank. The fire rose to the heaven, lighting up the sky. Carved into the sand were long deep furrows, which acted as makeshift seats, making the space look like an arena. Cushions, pillows and rugs were strewn around under trees and on side areas to allow for some privacy for new acquaintances.

As she moved further inside the dance area, she spotted them. Men. Hundreds of men of all ages and sizes stood around. A cheer went up as they saw the women entering the party area.

Ariel stood by the entrance, watching the women milling onto the dance floor. Some seemed to search for familiar faces who greeted them happily; other seemed as lost and cautious as she was.

She took in the scene as men began to mingle with women. Some already dancing in intimate poses, sandwiched between two partners. Others were already leading a partner or two away. The rest seemed more hesitant.

"First time?" a deep voice came from beside her. She jumped, turning towards the sound. "Sorry, I didn't mean to startle you," Ariel found herself staring at a dazzling smile and blazing blue eyes.

"It's fine. I'm fine." She recited her trusty mantra.

"Yes, you are." He showed his teeth again; his eyes traced her figure. "Well, is it?"

"What?"

"Your first time?"

"Yes, it is." Ariel bit her lip and played with the folds of her dress.

"Even better. Liam." He extended his hand to her as his eyes lingered on her bosom.

"Ariel." She extended her arm in return. He took it in his and pressed his lips to her skin. The sensation sent shivers down her spine and she snatched her hand back.

Liam chuckled. "Would you like a drink, Ariel?"

"Sure." Her voice sounded hoarse, and she found it hard to swallow.

Liam slunk his hand into hers and led her down beyond the dance floor and to the bar that stood opposite. He took two pints of honey ale and passed her a glass. Their glasses clinked and Liam downed half of his beer while Ariel sipped and put the near full glass back down.

"Dance?"

He didn't wait for her to answer but pulled her into his arms and maneuvered them into the middle of the dance floor. Bodies crashed around them as Liam held her in a firm clasp. Men and women danced and swayed, sweat and sex filling the air.

She could feel his large hand meandering down to her buttock where it rested, squeezing the flesh ever so subtly. She felt his soft lips on her nape as he whispered something, lost by the music.

"What?" She yelled over the music.

"Would you like me to show you around?" His eyes flickered with menace and lust.

"No, thanks. I think I'll just finish my drink." She tried to push away from him, but he maintained his hold on her, still moving against her. Ariel let her arms drop and stood limply in his arms. At this, he released his grip on her and stepped away, disappointment visible across his face. As he turned away from Ariel, a body smashed into his. The woman apologised and his scowl was replaced by a smile once more as he wrapped his hands around his more than willing new partner.

Ariel returned to the bar and reached for a fresh drink. She let the taste of honey wash down the taste of her failure, and watched the crowd, how they so easily fell into one another. She sucked at the beer once more, gulping at the liquid.

Once she had finished it, she took another and emptied the contents in half the time. If all she needed was courage, maybe she could find it at the bottom of a glass.

"I didn't take you for a drinker."

"I'm not." She slammed the glass on the bar.

"I can see." The newcomer chuckled.

"I don't usually drink at all." She reached for a third pint "But maybe tonight is a good time to start."

"And you've had how many?"

"This would be my third."

"And it's going to be your last if you have it."

"Is that right?'

"Yes, the drinks tonight are made extra strong. If you don't usually drink, you won't fare well."

Ariel stopped, the glass halfway to her mouth. The tingling of the previous two suddenly taking effect.

Her head buzzed and her legs felt like jelly as her stomach lurched.

"I don't feel so well."

"Here, let me get you out of here." He extended his hand to her.

"Not interested." She slapped it away.

"Of getting out of here?"

"Of being your mate."

"That's not what I offered."

"Oh." Her shoulders slumped as heat rose to her face. Humiliation gripped her as a strong hand wrapped itself around her upper arm and led her away from the bar and the dance area.

The sand felt soft under her feet as they crested the dune, distancing themselves from the dance floor. The music became muted and the sounds of waves crashing against rocks took over.

The man stopped and pointed to a rug strewn on the sand.

"Sit."

"No thanks."

"Okay, suit yourself." He released his grip on her and walked over to the rug. Ariel's wobbly legs folded beneath her and she hit the sand. She crawled to the rug and lay panting, her stomach churning.

"I don't feel so good."

"You don't look great, either."

"Who do you think you are?" She looked up for the first time, studying the man's face. His sun-kissed hair sat in a frenzied mop, falling across his forehead. His sharp chin was speckled with growth and his familiar brown eyes held the same humour as they always had.

"Ben?" As she uttered the word, vomit erupted from her throat. Thick, sticky honey ale covered the rug and most of his legs.

"Nice to see you, too, Ariel." He cringed and covered his nose when he got a whiff of hot vomit. He watched it drip and slog along his torso and between his legs.

"Oh god, I'm so sorry."

"Don't worry about it." His mouth cracked open like a fault line and rows of white teeth sparkled in the moonlight. "Now, if you don't mind -" He pointed to his legs and groin and stood up. "I'm going to go clean up."

Vomit leaked down his legs as he made his way towards the sea. Ariel watched his shape, silhouetted against the moonlight. He was wider and more defined, his sculpted chest like marble. Ben took off his white shirt and bent down to peel off his pants.

Ariel watched as he walked away, noting his strong back

and round buttocks. Once he had stripped down, he ran into the ocean, allowing the water to swallow him up. She watched as he scrubbed his legs and groin, pretending her body didn't respond at all to the sight of a naked man. This naked man.

Feeling a little better without the alcohol in her stomach, Ariel pulled herself up and shuffled to the sea line. Hot, lacy foam lapped at her feet. Ariel bent down to gather some in her hands, washing her face, the sea water, salty and warm, like a soup left out too long.

"For a moment there I thought you were going to join me." She looked up, her face in perfect line with Ben's groin. She thought for a moment about that day in the hidden pool. The game they played. When he showed her his, she remembered it looking much different. Thinner and hairless. She shuddered and turned around.

"Get that thing out of my face."

"I'd love to, but you puked on my only pair of pants so unless you plan on giving me your dress to cover up with, I guess you're stuck with this."

"That's not happening."

"Why? I showed you mine." He winked at her, his face splitting into a lopsided grin.

"And it still isn't much to look at." Ariel huffed.

"Oh? So you have thought of what it used to look like?" His grin widened and his eyes sparkled with mischief.

"No! I didn't say... that's not what I mea..." She hissed and threw her arms up the air and turned her back to him. Walking back up the beach, she looked for an escape. She heard his suppressed laughter as she trudged through the sand.

This was not how she had imagined their reunion. Ariel's mouth felt dry and her head was beginning to pound. Her heart was trying to break free from her chest and she knew that at least one of those things had nothing to do with honey ale.

"Accommodation is the other way." Ben cleared his throat. He had caught up and was walking quietly behind her.

"Yeah, I know. I just wanted some fresh air." Ariel met his eyes, aware that he was nude. She ground her jaw, willing her eyes to remain above his neckline.

"You're still a shit liar, Ariel," he said, his face parted in a smirk.

"I wasn't lying. I have a headache and I want to go lie down."

"And miss the party? It's the first night."

"So, who's stopping you from enjoying it, then?"

"You!"

"Me?"

"Yes, you." He crossed his arms, holding them across his chest.

"How?"

He raised an eyebrow. "Are you really asking me that?"

"Sorry I puked all over you. Now go find more pants or not, and enjoy the party. I'm a big girl now. I can look after myself."

"I've been waiting for you." His eyes grew wider as he studied her face.

She looked away, her eyes resting on the restless sea beyond. "No one asked you to."

"I've been waiting for you for five years. I really didn't think that after all this time it would be like this…" She heard the disappointment in his voice; it cut her like a sharp knife.

"Like I said, no one asked you to." Her voice wavered and she tugged on her dress.

"Ariel."

"Just go to the party and find a mate and have fun and leave me alone." She took a step back, unable to look at him.

"Ariel." He reached for her but she flinched away.

"Just go."

She didn't turn around as she marched up the beach towards the accommodation tents. She passed a number of couples drifting off into the forest and on to the beach. The sounds of moaning and low grunts filled the air. Ariel trudged on. She passed Liam who was alone once more. He nodded to her with a smile and she instantly regretted making eye contact with him.

He was already by her side. "Hi again."

"Hi."

"Where are you off to in such a hurry?"

"I'm going to bed."

"Are you now?" Liam seemed to have gotten a spring in his step.

Ariel ignored him for the rest of the walk, hoping he would get the hint, yet he remained. She reached the entrance to her tent and stopped.

"Good night." She raised the flap of the tent and walked inside.

"Oh, you do like playing hard to get, don't you?" Liam stood at the doorway, a hungry look in his eyes.

"I am not playing, Liam. I came here to sleep. You need to leave."

"What are you talking about? I am not leaving, not without getting something."

"And what exactly is it that you want?" She sighed.

"What do you think I want?" He stepped toward her, closing the distance between them.

"I don't know, but I want to go to sleep."

"That's not what you want." He took another step.

"Oh, no?"

"Why don't you take that dress of yours off and I'll show you what you need?" He took a final step, closing the distance between them, his body inches from hers. His hand surpassed her face and extended straight to her swollen breasts. His thumb found a nipple and circled it slowly.

Ariel bit her lip. She looked at Liam through long lashes and inhaled softly.

"No, thank you," Her knee connected with his groin. Ariel threw as much force into the blow as she could muster.

Liam squealed like a pig. His unwelcome hands falling from her bosom reached for his injured crotch. His knees buckled, meeting the sand with a soft thud as he fell in a crumpled mess. His face red with pain, he gasped for breath as if he was choking on the very air he was sucking in.

The flap of the tent flew open. Ben's face, followed by his still nude body, almost fell into the tent in his haste.

"Are you okay?" His eyes swept over the room, flicking from Ariel to Liam who lay curled up on the floor, concern melting into amusement.

"What are you doing here?" Ariel snapped, once again trying to keep her eyes above his chest.

"Well, that's no way to thank your rescuer."

"Does it look like I need to be rescued?" Her brows knitted in a frown.

"You bitch!" hissed Liam from the floor, who seemed to have remembered how to breathe.

"Watch your mouth, Liam." Ben's tone was stern.

"Mind your own business." Liam pushed himself up to a seated position while his knees were still firmly tucked to his chest.

"Make me."

"Ben!" Ariel gave him a look designed to peel his hide. "Get out! I don't need your help. And you, go with him. I said no, and I meant it. All I want is to sleep and I've been doing that all my life, so I don't need either of you to show me how." Ben's smile was back while Liam's face folded in a snarl.

Liam pushed himself to his feet and hobbled out, still hunched over.

Ben waited for him to leave then turned back to Ariel. "So, are you really going to bed now?"

Ariel placed a hand on Ben's chest, noting the soft skin and light peppering of dark hair. His skin was warm, pliant to her hand. She pushed hard at his chest, making him take a step back, her hand lingering longer than she had intended. Prying her eyes from his, she turned to her cot.

"Goodnight, Ben." Ariel lay on her cot and turned her back to Ben, who stood at the door seeming unsure. When Ariel made no other move, she heard him step out. She bit her lip, fighting tears. Bringing her knees up to her chest, she held herself tightly.

Ariel stared at the ceiling of her tent, the light blue the colour of sky. Listening to the music and human symphonies going on around her, she wondered why she felt so out of place. She fell asleep to thoughts of Ben and where the night would have taken him.

CONFESSION

W hen she woke up, Ariel felt the tiny tentacles of a headache. She knew it wouldn't be bad and was grateful that she had vomited the night before. Thinking of the scene on the beach, she grimaced and moaned, slapping a hand across her forehead and pulling it down, huffing.

Once her internal turmoil settled, she decided that breakfast would be a good way to start her day. Maybe some sunlight would help her find what everyone else had already seemed to work out.

She stepped out and tripped over a curled body which lay motionless at the entrance to her tent. As gracefully as a newly shorn sheep, she proceeded to trip, her scream catching in her throat as she hit the sand face first.

Ben groaned at the commotion but made no sign to move.

Ariel kicked him from her newly found position on the ground.

"Ow!" The still naked man sat up and rubbed his arm, "What was that for?" Fine white particles plastered his face and entire right side of his body. He looked at Ariel and burst out laughing. Her face covered in sand, she looked like a cracked porcelain doll who had come for revenge.

"What the hell, Ben?"

"What?"

"What are you doing here?"

"I was just…"

"Making sure no one else came in?" She finished the sentence for him.

He shrugged.

Ariel stood up. "I told you I don't need any help."

"I know, but I was hoping we could at least have some breakfast? You know? Catch up?"

"Fine," she huffed, "but not till you put that thing away." She couldn't help but stare, then pretended not to have been.

Ben patted the sand around him. He found the white pants that dried overnight. Standing up, he turned around giving Ariel another glimpse of his shapely buttocks as he slipped into his shorts. He turned around, a hand rubbing his face in an attempt to rid himself of the sand, and the smirk on his face.

A riel sat admiring her coffee. The hot amber liquid tasted too sweet, her dry throat welcoming the liquid. An infertile in slack brown robes placed breakfast in front of her, the smell making her feel queasy. She nodded her thanks as he walked off serving others. She had seen them, the community of the infertile. The Brown Robes. It was them who ran the island, who cooked meals and cleaned beds, who served alcohol, who helped The Watchers watch. They ensured the visitors had no chores, no duties and no worries, allowing them to focus on their one and only obligation.

"Sorry about last night." She looked into her cup as if all her answers awaited at the bottom of it.

"Don't be." Ben's nonchalance was simultaneously reassuring and annoying.

"But you didn't get to… you know…"

"Mate?"

"Yeah." She could feel the blush already rising to her cheeks.

"I have a week, Ariel. I'm sure I'll be fine."

"I'm sure you will," she mumbled into her coffee.

"So I was thinking –"

"Hope you didn't hurt yourself."

"-did you just? Really?" Ariel covered her smirk with a final gulp. Ben shook his head, amused. "As I was saying, I WAS THINKING –" He paused for effect. When she said nothing, he cleared his throat, "How about we go explore the island after breakfast?"

"Explore?"

"Yeah, like we used to back home, you know."

"Home? Inan hasn't been your home in years." Her eyes wandered over his features.

"Inan will always be home." There was a trace of melancholy, the words coming out as a mere whisper.

"Wouldn't you rather…" she gestured in a vague way, encircling her arms at the crowd, "you know?"

"I've already told you, I have a week and let's be honest. I don't think I'll have any trouble finding a mate." As if to reiterate his point he waved and winked at a circle of women who were eyeing him off, giggling. "See? Now, are you in or are you out?"

"Isn't that your job?"

They both burst out laughing.

They had walked along the length of the white shore, searching for a path that would lead them into the dense forest and beyond. A way to climb the untamed mountain that cast its long shadow above them.

"So, what do you do on Dagon?" Ariel wrung her wrist as her feet sank into the sand.

"Well, mainly the same thing as you, but no kids or babies to run around after. We hunt and fish. The daily boatload goes over to Inan and some of the other islands in the Quarter, as you know. When I was younger, when I just got there, I tried to sneak on it, you know so I could come and see you and my mom again but turns out I wasn't very good at hiding." He snickered to himself.

Ariel chuckled, sizing him up.

"I wasn't always this big…"

"No, but you've always been this goofy."

"Hey." He shoved her with his shoulder, pushing her aside.

For the first time, she noticed the curved groves lining Ben's back. Like a bursting snake pit writhing and slithering across his back.

"Is that how you got those?"

He nodded. "There's always a price to pay…" He didn't elaborate.

He cleared his throat and Ariel pried her eyes away. "So what did you have to do then?"

"I am a builder. Turned out hunting and gathering wasn't my thing, I was more a giver of shelter and protection."

"You sound like a great catch." She smirked.

"What's wrong with building a shelter?"

'Nothing – I am sure it would be a beautiful place to starve in." Her grin widened.

"I won't starve."

"How's that?" She raised a single eyebrow.

"I'll have you bringing all the fish home."

"Will you now?" The brow rose further.

He stopped in his tracks, a gleam of mischief in his eye as he looked down into her eyes. "Your mom is the elder. She can always appoint you a fisherwoman."

"I guess she could." She nodded.

"Well, I don't see the problem, then."

"And who would look after the kids while I'm out fishing all day?" She played along.

"Kids? So, we are having more than one?"

"*We* are having none. Pretty sure I have told you, you are not coming anywhere near me with that monstrosity between your legs." She began walking again.

"Oh, so it's a monster now?" he teased. "It might be big, but it's not very scary…"

"Pretty sure you have it the wrong way around."

"Hey!" he called after her as she bolted ahead, knowing she would pay for her last remark.

He tackled her to the ground and they fell rolling, white particles sticking to their moist skins. Tucked beneath him, Ariel tried to squirm away from his touch, but his body, much larger and heavier than hers, held her down.

"Let me go." She squealed, her body fighting fits of giggles as Ben grabbed her hands, forcing them over her head.

"Surrender."

"Never."

Ben pushed her down, holding her body in place. Hair covered her face and he took a second to snigger at her effort to blow it out of her mouth.

"Surrender," Ben whispered into her ear, his soft lips grazing the thin skin on her neck. Her body stilled with the huskiness of his voice. A shiver ran down her spine as coarse fingers under a gentle touch swept hair away from her face. Ariel's heart pounded as she studied his face. Her eyes roamed his stubbly cheekbones, his lips, his chocolate brown eyes, intent and unwavering.

His wild hair fell across his forehead as he pressed himself to her, his lips inches from her own. She gasped, feeling his chest rise and fall in unison with her own. His coffee breath lingered as a warmth settled across her body. Her heart galloped as her breath became quicker.

She squirmed once more beneath him. Her body bucked and Ben rolled off her, laying in the sand, his chest rising and falling in a frenzy.

Ariel shot up and shook the sand from her body catching her breath. "Coming?"

"Not now, I guess," he mumbled under his breath.

"What's that?"

He shook his head and jumped up, spraying a fine mist of sand everywhere as he shook it off.

Ariel spotted a break in the greenery and headed for the opening, pretending not to notice the awkwardness of Ben's stride or the change in the shape of his pants.

They walked in silence for a while, the swooshing of branches and crunching of gravel following them.

"How is Rosalie?" Ben asked, breaking the silence between them.

"She is not the same." Ariel considered her words. "She has two boys."

"Oh."

"She's come to terms with it." She didn't look at Ben as she spoke.

They ploughed through the rough path, the ascent starting off slowly, easily. Soon the gravel path gave way to hard rock and firm brown soil that sank into the ground.

Without realising, they had fallen into old habits and began competing. Both increasing their pace, an elbow here to push a little forward, a shove there to gain some ground.

They had reached a stone face with an oval cavern. The

perfect, smooth edges evidently handmade. A carved path wormed through the mountain and allowed access to its peak. The pair stepped inside, loose pebbles crunching underfoot.

"Shhh." Ben halted, extending a hand blocking Ariel's advance.

"Ben, what –"

"Shhh." Then she heard it, too. A scuffling in the rock as if it was being scratched from inside. The noise emanated from just beyond the stone wall.

The pair looked at one another, each daring the other to go investigate. As one, they stepped forward and rounded the wall.

"What the hell, man? Can we get some privacy please?" The man, leaned back on the rock wall, his torso exposed, his hands laced through a woman's thick black hair. She rested on her knees before him, his hands guiding her head. Despite the interruption, they did not stop.

Ariel felt the crimson tide washing over her features as she turned and bolted from the tunnel.

Ben exited shortly after, a wide grin on his face. "Don't like to watch?"

"Do you? Maybe you need lessons?"

"I don't need lessons from anyone." He stood like a peacock in plumage.

Ariel closed the distance between them, pushing against his strong chest, forcing him against the cold wall. She traced his face with a delicate touch, pinning him with her gaze, as she pressed herself against him. Her face inches from his. She brushed his lips with hers, not quite a kiss but a promise that there would be more to come. The single tinge travelled from her mouth down the length of her body, exploding in her navel and below. She felt his body react, the stiffened muscles, the held breath.

"You know," she whispered in his ear, her voice husky, "I

may not know much, but I am fairly sure, that was the wrong hole…"

Ariel stepped back, a smirk painted on her face. Ben remained against the wall breathless for a second more, before his face broke into a wild grin.

They found shelter from the hot, relentless sun. Their feet dangled from the cliff face as they watched the landscape below.

"Do you miss your mom?"

"Sometimes."

"I can send her a message if you want."

"You'd do that?"

"Of course."

"What would I even tell her? I haven't seen her in five years."

"I'll just tell her you said hi and you miss her. I think she'd like that."

"I think she would, too."

They sat there for a while longer watching the island, spotting couples. In the bushes and the brush, on the beach and in the forest. Before deciding to leave, they had counted over sixty men and women copulating in one way or another.

"I'm getting too hot. Let's head down for a swim." He didn't wait for her to answer but simply stood up and retraced his steps towards the tunnel.

Catching up to him, Ariel sidestepped around him and ran right by him, the hollow nook that was previously occupied now empty. Ben chased her all the way to the beach, allowing her to win.

Panting, they stood at the water's edge.

"I'm going in. Are you coming?"

"Think I'll sit out." Ariel retreated.

"Why?"

"Because –" She bit her lip and instinctively covered her body with her arms. "I just don't want to…" She gestured at her body.

"But you're beautiful, Ariel."

"I've never been beautiful." Ariel's eyes wandered across the hot yellow sand.

"You've never stopped." The muscles in his cheeks flexed and he ran a hand through his hair. "What if I hold your hand and look straight ahead? I won't peek. Also, if anyone does look this way, they will see us together and think we're together. They won't bother you."

"But if they think we're together then – "

"I know…" He shifted his weight on the sand.

"But then you won't get to – "

"I still could. With as many as I wanted to."

"Ben. I don't want to be your mate. I don't think I'm ready to mate with anyone." She wrung her wrist, avoiding his eyes.

"Then I'll wait for you. Like I have been."

"Ben…"

"Will you just come swimming with me already?" He threw his hands up.

"Fine." She frowned. "But keep that water snake away from me…"

"Oh, so he's a snake now?" He wiggled his eyebrows, his face lit up in a boyish grin.

"Shut up." She giggled.

Ben placed both thumbs beneath the band of his pants and removed them then stepped behind Ariel to help her with her clasp.

"You will look straight ahead?" Her voice quivered.

"Promise."

Ben unclasped the ring of Ariel's dress and watched the soft fabric cascade down her tanned body. The curves like tumbling waves, perfect. He gasped. She felt his eyes on her, and knew that if she looked into them, she will find only desire. Instead, he stepped away giving her his hand and she knew he would keep his promise. She laced her fingers into his then led them in a sprint into the water.

They were both laughing when they fell into the waves. Coming up for air, Ben studied her. Droplets fell from her brown hair which stuck to her face. Her dimples dipped as she smiled at him. Her long neck protruded from beyond the water and his fingers itched to trace it down to her navel. He noticed the swell of her breasts and the pink tips as they stood erect just below the water.

The splash came out of nowhere. Salt water rushed into his mouth and across his face.

"Stop staring or your eyes will fall out." She giggled.

"That's an old wives' tale." He wiped water from his eyes.

"No such thing."

"What?"

"An old wife. Any wife, really."

He frowned, trying to understand her meaning as another splash sprayed across his body.

"What was that for?"

"That one was because I can," she teased.

"Well, you get those two for free, but once more, and there is no telling what this water snake will do."

"It would have to catch me first." She giggled, knowing she could outswim him. On land he might be master but, in the ocean, there would be no beating her.

Instead he stood up and headed to shore.

"Hey, where are you going?"

"Think I've cooled down enough, and anyway I promised to look away on the way in. We never said anything about the way out." He gave her a wicked smile as he trudged through the swelling waves.

"Ben! Ben, you come back here!" When she saw he wasn't

turning back, she sprinted to catch up with him, water splashing widely in her wake as she tried to cover up and run. Once she was safely behind him, she allowed herself to breathe and followed his larger form inland, allowing it to shield her.

They reached their clothes. Ben kept his back to her and she was grateful for his gift to her.

He didn't look at her as he slipped into his pants. "There will be another party tonight, and the night after that. Are you going to stay in your tent the whole time?"

"What else is there to do?"

"Come dance with me."

Ariel frowned at him then turned around, indicating that he should clasp her dress back up.

He traced his fingers along her shoulder, her wet skin breaking in goosebumps at his touch. Pulling the dress shut, he held on to the thin cloth. "Everyone will think we are together. I told you, you can have fun, worry free. No other guy will make a move as long as you're with me."

"But what about you?" She spun out of his reach.

"I told you, I'll be fine."

"You've already wasted a whole day with me."

"When will you realise, Ariel, that time with you is not wasted? Not where I am concerned."

His remarks shut down any further protests and she agreed to meet him later for a dance and a drink.

When they arrived at Ariel's tent, Ben leaned into the cool blue structure. "Do I need to take my nap outside your tent again?" He arched a sly brow.

"I'm pretty sure I can take care of myself!"

"You know what? I am pretty sure you can, too." He gave her a wink, sending her heart aflutter. When at last he left and the flap dropped behind him, Ariel sank to her cot. Pain creased her face, her insides constricted in misery.

When evening crept in, the drums started to beat. The rhythm echoed across the entire island, enticing its inhabitants to come out of their shelters and back to the central area where bodies clashed once more in dance.

She exited her tent and saw the dying light in the sky. The yellow ball of fire had changed to hues of orange, fighting black tentacles as night beckoned the stars. Music filled the air like a fine mist. She followed its trail like a treacherous wave.

When she arrived, swarms of people were already on the dance floor. Bodies in motion, twisting, turning, fused together like a multi-headed beast.

Her chest tightened as she spotted Ben. She took a long steadying breath, admonishing herself for allowing him to make her feel this way. He was leaning against the bar. His bare chest, in full view, glowed under the strobing lights. He wore a grin as white as his pants, as two blondes competed for his affection. Fingers twirling in hair, bosoms on full show, they sipped and giggled. Ariel watched, fascinated, as he held their attention. They were completely captivated by him. She could almost admit to herself that she knew why.

It was when one of the blondes placed her hand on his and her fingers brushed the skin of his arm that Ariel advanced toward the small group.

Ben spotted Ariel and broke away from the other two, excusing himself. Their gaze tracked him wistfully as he greeted Ariel with a broad smile.

"Didn't think you were coming," he shouted over the music.

"The music just started. Anyway, I have been here for ages. It's you that's been otherwise occupied."

"With them?" He thumbed behind him at the blondes who

were now arm in arm with two new men. "Just kept myself entertained till my real date showed."

"And by 'entertained' you mean?"

"Do you really want to know?" He wiggled his eyebrows wildly.

"Oh, shut up." She giggled. "So, are you going to get me a drink?"

"After last night's performance? I think not."

"Ppfft" She pushed past him and grabbed a pint of honey ale from the bar. She sipped on the warm beer.

"Take it easy now."

"Yes, Mother," she teased and gulped the rest of the drink, smacking the glass down on the bar as she finished.

"Or not." He shrugged. "Dance?"

"Sure." Her eyes sparkled as she grabbed him by the hand. It was clammy and slippery. She felt his grip tighten around her fingers as she cleaved her way through a mass of bodies towards the middle of the dance floor.

Bodies crashed against them, pushing them against one another, their sweat-clad bodies slippery, the sweat making the fabric cling to her body, showing off her figure and all that lay beneath.

Her mouth felt dry as his hand dug into her flesh, pulling her closer. Bodies rubbing, lashing and beating against them to the strumming of the music, lust and sex hung in the air as couples kissed and touched in a frenzy.

She clung to him, her body teaming with sweat and want and desire and fear of all that that meant. She wrapped her arms around him, forcing their bodies to move as one, entangled limbs and fluid motion.

The rhythm took on a frenzied pace. The crowd cheered and danced as if crazed with the night and the drink and the lust. Ben slid his hand along her slick back, and the crowd closed in on them, pushing them ever closer until there was nowhere to go but into one another. Ariel's face was inches from his. His hair was pasted to his face. Ben looked into her eyes, his penetrating gaze unwavering as one corner of his mouth lifted in a half-grin.

Before she could stop him, she felt his lips brush hers. She gasped and jerked her head back. Ben did not release her, instead weaving a hand through her hair, pulling her closer, clutching her tighter. Her heart threatened to break through her chest as it heaved. Without thinking, her lips were on his, urgent and needy. The stolen kiss from years back, his to return and hers to claim. But they were not thirteen anymore and the kiss was not innocent. It was fire and wilderness and lust and need all mixed into one. Years of pent-up desire spilled in a tangled frenzy of tongues. She drowned in his skin and his touch, and when she broke away, she saw Ben for the first time. And all that he meant to her. And all that he would ever mean to her.

Ariel stared at him for a single minute before turning away and carving her way through the throng of bodies leaving him there like an island whose shores were being battered.

Ben caught up with her just before she reached her tent, grabbing her arm and spinning her around.

He held up his hand as he caught his breath and took her in. The wild hair, her hard nipples, her curvy shape. "What was that?'

"A mistake."

"That wasn't a mistake." His brow creased, his voice raising.

"It can't happen again."

"What the hell, Ariel? Don't tell me you don't feel it, too."

"We can't, I just can't." She pivoted on her heels and marched away.

Ben chased her down and blocked her path. "Why? What's so wrong with me? With us?" He sliced the air with a clenched fist.

"Everything." She sighed "We can't, I won't."

"Just tell me why, and I will leave you alone. I won't hurt you, Ariel."

"Can't you see? That is exactly what you will be doing."

"What are you talking about?" The cords of his neck stretch taut.

"I don't want to end up like Rosalie."

"I don't understand." He reached for her arm, but she flinched away.

Ariel looked down and bit her lip, her eyes glistening with tears.

"Ariel?" he tried again, taking her hand in his. It remained limp.

"If we do this, I will lose you all over again," she whimpered.

"No." He searched for her eyes. "Ariel, we can...'

"No!" she cut him off, pulling her hand from his. "We can't." Her tone was final and with that, she left him standing on the beach and made her way back to her tent.

Her heart raced as she broke into her tent, her lower lip quivering, the flap, a thin barrier between her and Ben. As she fought her body, which ached to be in his arms, she reminded herself of the cost. Staggering to the sunken bed, she collapsed and finally let the tears run.

12

PLAN

A riel knew that she would have no choice. If she was not seen to be doing her duty, she would be reported. There would be consequences. Yet the one person she wanted, she didn't dare go near and he, in turn, returned the favour. When she woke, he was not outside her door as she had found herself hoping. She did not see him at breakfast nor along the empty dance floor that seemed alive the night before.

When she did spot him, she winced. Ben was surrounded by a gaggle of women on the beach. Ariel pretended her heart didn't pang when they stroked or touched him. When they ran fingers through his hair, along his navel, across his lips.

She didn't want to imagine what Ben might be doing and with who. She knew she couldn't keep hiding in her tent. The Watchers would know. They would report.

Maybe she could get away with being alone, untouched, for just one more day.

She walked along the beach, looking for sanctuary. Five more days to survive and go home. Where she could be safe for three more months before having to return.

She spotted the group of masked men surrounding The Watcher. Clad in red, the old woman stood out against the golden sand. The Watcher eyed Ariel as she walked leisurely along the beach. The Watcher's mouth stretched in a grin and she patted the sand next to her and waited until Ariel sat down by her side.

"All alone?" Her voice was sweet. The folds of her skin rippled with the motion.

"I needed time to think."

"Indeed, this place can make a girl dizzy, so many dicks and not a man in sight." The old lady cackled at her own joke. "Have you been enjoying yourself?"

"It's been interesting."

"That is an interesting choice of words." It was a statement, not a question, and yet Ariel felt compelled to explain.

"It's not what I was expecting."

"And what were you expecting, dear? Have you not been briefed? Did your mother not explain?"

"I was, and she did."

"So, what seems to be the problem?"

Ariel sighed, not knowing how much she should say. "There is no problem."

"No?'

"No."

"So why is it that you have not mated yet?"

"Who said that?"

"Have you?"

"I don't think that's any – "

"Let me stop you there, dear." The friendly voice had turned cold. "I am the Watcher Tay, daughter of Audrey, and indeed it is my business to know what goes on, on this island. Whatever reservation you have, dear girl, remember that they are irrelevant. You are a vessel, a tool, and nothing more. There should be no feelings, or qualms, or fear. Spread your legs and let them do all the work. If you are lucky, it will be over quickly, and if you are luckier, it will not." The old woman grinned at the last as if thinking of a pleasant dream. "If you do not claim a mate by your sixth day, one or more will be claimed for you." She pointed at the masked soldiers who leered at Ariel, sending a cold shiver up her spine. "You know the rules, girl. Do your duty, or one of my fine gentlemen here might take you." She winked at the three soldiers who took a step closer.

"Stop it, Tay, you're scaring the girl. She still has plenty of time to do what needs to be done." The silver-haired man sauntered in their direction, a frown marring his gentle face. Ariel did not see where he had come from.

"We were just having a chat, no need to worry, Eric." Her tone was singsong once more.

"Indeed." He nodded his head slightly and studied Ariel intently.

"Get on with it, girl." The Watcher waved her off, a tone of nonchalance back.

Without a word, Ariel shot up and made her way towards the main beach, which was infested with bodies.

Trudging back along the yellow sand, her eyes scanned the coastline, pretending not be seeking out Ben. She spotted him. A red-haired woman was leaning into his body, her hands in his hair, her lip glistening. She leaned in further, her lips puckering, and as she tilted her head to his, Ben turned away. Her kiss landed on his cheek.

Ariel inhaled a breath she didn't realise she was holding and left the beach, her footsteps feeling a little lighter on the sand.

G oing to the mess hall for some lunch she pretended that the pain in her chest was the bad breakfast she ate that morning.

As the day wore on, it became more difficult to avert the advances of her many pursuers. It was as if word had spread of her reluctance and that made it a challenge for the men, like a rare flower to be plucked from wuthering heights. She would not yield, and their advances, although amusing at times, got tiring.

"Why so glum?"

"Who's glum? I am having the time of my life, just like everyone said I would be." She didn't look at Ben as she spoke, preferring to watch the ocean over her mug of coffee.

"I can see that. You have 'party' written all over your face."

"And you have saliva all over yours." She almost spat the words.

"Jealous?" A smirk pushed its way to the corner of his mouth.

"Of those girls? No."

"Oh, but you are jealous. How many girls did you see?"

"Shouldn't you be behind a bush somewhere sticking that sausage in someone?"

"So we are at food items now? Does that mean you'd like a taste?"

The statement made her look at him for the first time. His face was full of mirth. "I've told you a hundred times, I don't want that thing anywhere near me and certainly nowhere near my mouth."

"Who said anything about putting it in your mouth? But if you want to, I won't stop you..." Ariel got up and walked away without a word. Ben jumped up behind her and caught up.

"Hey, I was just joking."

"I know." She didn't stop.

"I didn't do anything with any of them."

"It's none of my business," she said, masking a hint of relief.

"It could be." He pivoted, blocking her way.

"I thought I made myself clear." She tried to push by him, but he sidestepped her, denying her escape.

"I guess I haven't made myself clear yet." He stood in her way, no longer acting like a fool. His chest out, Ben stood to his full height, his thick hair like wild fire dancing across his face in the breeze and his chiseled jaw tight as he clenched it.

"Why do you think this is only about you, and what you want? I know it's your body, but it will be growing my child, or someone's child." His face grew taut. "Do you have any idea of the enormity and weight that bears? I know you know what life is like without a father, but do you understand how painful it is at thirteen to lose your mother as well?" The muscles on his face and neck stood rigid as his jaw clenched.

"Oh Ben." She approached him, but he stepped back.

"Why do I have to oblige to give a part of me to any of these women? They will forever take that piece away and I will have nothing to do with it. You have no idea how many nights I stayed up crying, missing my mom. Brought up by strangers with different rules, different hierarchies. A man's world is unlike yours." His voice strained as he choked back tears, his finger tracing a tentacle of scar which hugged his hip.

"Turns out my mom liked to have fun." He sneered. "It was a costly exercise for me to find out all of my mother's mates. It took three years to compile all that information. When I did find the potential candidate, he was Shuffled four years before my arrival. Records show he died a year later in the Second Quarter. The man who had brought me into the world gone - and I know nothing about him except that he was a good swimmer, and I am not, and that he probably died alone and surrounded by strangers. I will die never knowing if I have anything in common with him, and I will die never seeing my mother again."

He took a deep breath to steady himself and ran his hands

down his pained face, pulling at the taut skin. "Why would I want to bring a child into this world knowing I would never see their face or hold their hand? Never teach him or her how to swim or dance or build a fire. Never tell them how beautiful their mother is and that I have loved her since the first day I saw her."

Ariel's mouth parted slightly at the words and Ben's rant softened, his harsh tone lowering to almost a whisper.

He stalked forward and placed Ariel's hand on his chest. "If I give a piece of me to someone, I'd rather it be my heart, and you already took a piece with you many years ago on that mountain in Inan." He closed the distance between them. His towering shape loomed over her as he wrapped a hand around her slim waist, the other stroking her chin. His light fingers wound through her hair and he grabbed a handful, gently tugging, forcing her to look into his eyes. Pinning her with a deafening look.

They stood as if frozen. The cords of his neck stretched taut, his mouth inches from her own. She swallowed hard, the feel of him around her like a safety net. She pushed herself on tiptoes and closed the distance between them, slamming her lips into his. Possessing him with a frenzied kiss. She pressed herself to him as her whole body screamed for more of his softness. Groaning, he tightened his hold as he deepened the kiss, his tongue sliding beyond the barriers of her soft lips.

When he released her, they stood for a moment, looking into each other's eyes. Ariel pushed him away, breathless. Tousled hair and crimson cheeks, Ben's eyes held a fiery look, she knew could set her alight.

"We can't, not if we both feel this way." Her eyes fell away and all hope vanished from her voice.

"But there is no way we can't not."

She nodded, tears welling in her eyes. "Doing this will

only bring us pain. You will break me. This will bring us only sorrow."

"No."

"Yes, if I fall pregnant…"

"So don't."

"Ben…"

"Maybe we can, but not really?" He pushed his hair out of his face and rubbed his jaw.

"What do you mean?"

Ben sat down and tapped his side, letting Ariel fall into the fine sand. He wrapped an arm around her and let her head rest onto his chest.

"We can pretend," he whispered.

"Pretend what?"

"We can pretend that we are mates. We can fake it, and then we can be together."

Ariel pushed away from him and studied his face. There was no trace of humour in his creased features. "How?"

"We can work out the," he cleared his throat, "logistics later. But the important thing is that if you don't fall pregnant, you have to come back. We both do. You have five rounds before you are deemed barren…"

His words begun to make sense in the fog of her mind.

"And you won't try to…?"

"I would never hurt you, Ariel, not now, not ever. We would only ever do what you want. You have the power, remember?"

"Do I now?" She looked at him, a quirky smile on her face, her eyebrows wiggling before she pushed him into the sand and mounted him.

"Seems to me as if you are in total control," he coaxed then bucked, the action making her lose her balance. In a swift, agile movement, Ben grabbed Ariel and flipped her onto her back then mounted her, his face inches from hers.

"Total control," he whispered into her ear and peppered

soft kisses down her neck, trailing her jawline and coming to a stop at her lips.

It was then Ben saw a pair of feet not a meter away from them. Looking up, he traced the feet up to see an old silver-haired man, whose hazel eyes were creased at the corners.

Ariel looked up and met his eyes.

"Good," the old man said, nodded, and walked away.

When he was out of earshot, Ben whispered, "See, we are doing it already."

"Doing what?"

"Fooling everyone."

They lay on the beach, soaking in the last of the rays, hands laced together as Ariel wondered if they were also fooling themselves.

"They are watching us," he whispered, kissing her cheek. "I know."

"It's 'cause neither of us..."

"I know..."

"So, we have to pretend to..."

"I know, I know." Ariel sighed.

"Where do you want to go?"

"I don't know."

"Well, that's unusual, isn't it?"

She threw a kernel of corn at his direction and finished chewing. "How about the caves?"

"The caves? They are far and dark."

"Exactly. They are dark and isolated. It will be harder to see, harder for them to be certain."

"Okay, but we will have to head out soon. We will have to spend the night there. We won't be able to come back down once night falls."

They packed some provisions and weaved their way to

the caves. A nervous energy flowed between them, neither talking much as they ascended the path, making their way to the rocky rooms above.

They lit their torches as they arrived at the entrance. Ben walked ahead, scanning the makeshift rooms. The only sounds his echoing footsteps as they crunched loose rock and the crackling of hay.

"It's empty."

"Good." Ariel bit her lip and took a tentative step inside the cave. Taking a long breath, she followed the glow of Ben's torch deeper into the worming tunnel.

She set her bag on the floor, pulling out her blanket and pillow and laying them on the ground, then rummaged in Ben's sack and found his. She set it next to hers while he built a small fire. Their jobs complete, they sat in silence, listening to twigs snap in the fire.

"Can I ask you something?"

"Sure." She gave him a small smile.

"Why do you keep saying you don't want to end up like Rosalie? What happened to her?"

Ariel sighed, her eyes focused somewhere beyond the yellow flames. "Rosalie is depressed."

"She's depressed?"

"All the time. She has two boys. Wayne is two and Max is almost five." Ariel's face lit up as she thought of her nephews. "They are handsome and so sweet. They have Rosalie's big eyes and thick black hair, and the rest, I guess, belongs to their father."

"*One* father?"

Ariel nodded absentmindedly. "She only mated with one man. She loved him."

"And he...?"

"Made her promises."

"What sort of promises?"

"The ones that end up in heartbreak and lies."

"Ariel?"

"He told her he loved her. The first time they met, Chris devoted himself to her. They were together and she spent her first visit here with him. He swore she had his heart and that if she fell pregnant and he had to be with others, he would force himself to be with a single mate while thinking of Rosalie." Ariel quaffed. "It was a ridiculous promise to make."

"He may have meant it."

"Sure." She scoffed.

"So what happened when she came back?"

"She had Max first. He was her pride and joy and she couldn't wait to tell Chris about his son. When she returned to Ishmin, she looked for him. And she found him, in the arms of another. She understood he didn't know she would return, so she forgave him." Ariel shook her head.

"She had spent two years thinking of only him, pining for her lover, as her body grew and changed and healed."

Tears glistened in Ariel's eyes as she thought of her sister. "She waited before she approached him. When she did, she said he didn't even recognise her. Again she forgave him and reminded him of all they had, of all they shared. Rosalie said that he said he remembered. He took her to his bed again for just one night. I guess that's when they made Wayne. The following day when she went to look for him, he was with another. She confronted him, and he laughed in her face. He told her he was never in love but only in lust, that her body was so delicious he would have said anything just to have a taste, but that it was broken now, a used thing and he wanted someone younger, better, more suitable to be *his* mate." Ariel almost spat out the words.

"When she came back, she was broken. She carried Wayne, and Mama Beth had her move back to the house. She wasn't taking care of herself or the boys." Ariel's face twisted in a grimace.

"She loved Chris and she lost him and, worst still, she

believed all his cruel words. One day she will lose both her sons. And the thought is killing her. Slowly."

"I can't imagine Rosalie sad."

"It's heart-breaking to watch. She isn't who she used to be."

"And if we do this, will you be the same?"

Ariel didn't answer, choosing instead to watch the fire. She lay down on the soft blanket, which offered a thin barrier between her body and the harsh rocks beneath. She studied Ben's face as the fire licked and kissed his features, highlighting his strong jaw and perfect lines. He came to lay by her and wrapped his arm around her, doing nothing more.

She had all the power.

Ariel turned to him, taking his face in her hands. She trailed a finger like a soft feather hovering just on the edge of his skin. She traced the shape of his jaw and neck, his shoulders and torso and back again.

"Stop." His face was rigid as if he was in pain.

"But I like touching you."

"Please stop. I don't think I can take it."

"This was your idea," Ariel teased.

"I know. I just didn't know it would be so hard." He ran a hand through his hair.

"You can touch me, but do not attempt to get under my clothes."

Following her lead, he traced the shape of her, taking his time, allowing his fingers to absorb her warmth as they touched her soft flesh and all that lay beneath the fabric, her soft curves yielding to his fingers.

Ariel wriggled into his arms and brushed his warms lips, coaxing them towards her. She pressed her mouth to his, his response desperate and fluid. Breaking away from him, she peppered kisses along his skin, tasting him for the first time. He tasted like sweat and salt and need. The flavour foreign yet delicious, a combination made just for her palate. She kissed his chest and arms, making her way down to the lining of his pants then back again. She could see his need for her and wished she could give herself more freely to him.

"We need to stop," she said through rasping breaths.

"We need to finish."

"I don't understand." She looked at him quizzically. "You promised." A note of fear in her voice.

Pushing himself away from her, he gave her a dark look. "Don't look at me like that. I've already told you I will never hurt you."

"I know… I'm sorry."

He huffed and rested on his elbow. "I know you think we may be alone, but we are being watched. We have to make it look like…." His faced stretched, willing her to understand.

Pursing her lips, she nodded and lay on her back, allowing him to blanket her body with his. Pretending to play with his pants, he adjusted himself and looked into her eyes. "I'm sorry, Ariel. I'll try and make it quick."

She nodded. Her pulse screamed as she felt him, his gentle movements above her stirring more than just desire. Heat and friction rose inside her and goosebumps erupted on her skin, as only a thin layer of fabric separated him from her. Her legs clenched against his hips as he rocked against her. His mouth collided into hers in urgent need, and when he pulled away, his gaze pinned her as it contorted, his jaw clenched. He shut his eyes and groaned into her neck as she felt the expanding warm pool on her belly.

He lay on top of her for a few minutes more, regaining his composure. "Sorry." He fell off her in a heap. Satisfaction and confusion marred his features.

"I'm not sure how to feel right now." He rubbed his face with his hands.

"What do you mean?"

"I mean I have been waiting for this moment for five years and it was nothing like how I hoped it would be."

She bit her lip, biting down her disappointment. "Sorry I can't be more for you."

"You never need to be more, Ariel. You're already everything." He kissed her shoulder, but she did not turn back to him, her eyes pooling with tears.

With a hand resting across her waist, he fell quickly asleep, as she stared at the fire, seeing their future burn.

13

CONSEQUENSES

D awn broke and the darkened sky softened to a light blue, shimmering rays colouring the world. The air grew warmer with a breeze blowing from the south. Ariel peeled herself away from Ben's still body, his mouth slightly ajar as he lay motionless in a deep slumber.

She rubbed sleep from her eyes and ignored the setting dread, that, like a lump of clay, had settled in the pit of her stomach. The Watchers seemed satisfied with their show two nights prior, and had left them alone. The old man was sure to make a quick visit as if to assure them they had passed some kind of test. At sunset, they would have to bid each other farewell.

She watched Ben sleep. His chest rose and fell like the swell of the ocean, his unruly sun-kissed hair framing his peaceful features. Ever so slowly, she raised her hand and traced his stubbled jawline, traces of growth covering the usually shaved surface. Ben's face twitched and he turned to his side, his large body sagging in her too small cot.

The sound of a horn resonated across the island, shaking Ariel from her daze and waking Ben. He groaned, stretching his body, as he awkwardly stumbled from the cot and onto the sand.

"What's that?" His voice was groggy with sleep and he cleared his throat.

"I'm not sure."

Ben brushed fingers through his hair, tucking strands behind his ears, then rubbed the sleep from his eyes. He stood, stretching. Though Ariel tried, she could not unglue her eyes from his body.

"Like what you see?" he teased when he caught her looking.

"Meh."

"Meh? Meh?" He stepped towards her, a menacing grin on his face. Ariel stepped back, a shriek escaping her. "I'll show you meh." He dived and she sidestepped him, giggling, his fingers brushing her skin. He pivoted, his face a mask of delight, his eyes hungry, focused.

Before he had another chance to pounce, the horn sounded once more, its heavy forlorn sound falling across Ishmin like a thick fog.

"We better go." All mirth gone from his features, he opened the flap of the tent and peered outside. "We are being summoned."

"We?" Her heart fell, skipping a beat.

"Everyone," he corrected and held out his hand to her.

Ben led them toward the gathering area, which no longer looked like a dance floor. The bar was gone, and in its place stood a raised platform. The entire population of the island had gathered and were standing in wait.

From the wings, the stage filled with men and women well past their youth. Most wore little but saggy skins and grey hair. They marched on, led by a man and a woman which Ariel instantly recognised.

The woman wore a long red dress. It flowed from her body and flapped easily in the breeze. Her long, white hair billowed behind her as she stepped forward. Her physique and stride didn't betray her age.

Next to her, walking as her equal was the man. He stood somewhat taller than her, his silver hair thick and full on his crown. A silver shadow covered his face as it lined his strong jaw.

"I am The Watcher Tay, daughter of Audrey. Beside me stands the Watcher Eric, son of Clara." The crowd fell silent as her soft melodious voice carried easily over them.

"We thank you for accepting our invitation and joining us this week to fulfill your duties as vessels and instruments of growth and reproduction." Ariel huffed as Ben squeezed her hand, urging her to remain quiet.

"On this seventh day, we must take stock, for tonight you shall all depart. Some of you never to return while others to grace us with your presence once more." Her smile stretched across her face like an elastic band stretched to its limits.

A shallow murmur rose in the crowd and she raised her hand, waiting for silence.

"Before your arrival, you were told of our rules. And we thank you, well, most of you for keeping them." Much to Ariel's dismay, her mouth stretched further still, her lips now almost invisible.

"As you know, our society exists and grows because we follow the rules set by our ancestors. They had seen the path to survival and prosperity, and with their guidance we obey. Yet, some seem to have become lost sheep and today we will guide them once more in the righteous path."

She looked to Eric who nodded. His eyes flickered somewhere beyond the crowd.

Four guardsmen ushered a man onto the raised platform. An eerie silence fell on the gathered visitors.

The man whose face was drawn and eyes sunken was dragged to the front of the stage. Once there, the soldiers pushed him onto his knees then cuffed his wrists in heavy metal chains behind his head. The opposite side of the chain was attached, with a final click, to a ring in the stage floor. Ariel studied him, vulnerable and naked, terror etched into every line of his face as his eyes sought rescue in the crowd.

Tay continued. "Before us comes Daniel, son of Annabelle. He is accused of breaking the rules. His accuser Celie, Daughter of Delia, as witnessed by The Watcher Inez. Daniel, you have been found guilty of force without kindness, of strength without control, and you shall be marked an abomination."

"No!" The man started to wiggle against his restraints. The two guardsmen by his side stood unaffected as if he was but a cool breeze whipping between them. "No! She did not object! It was not forced," he yelled, the clanging of his metal cuffs reverberating through the silent audience.

Tay smirked as Eric singled, and a third guard stepped on the stage. In his hand, he held a long branding rod, on its end a round circle holding within it the letter A. The encapsulated letter blazed white with the heat.

The captured man begged, thrashing against his restraints. He looked to Tay as he pleaded, she did not show him empathy.

"Proceed." She spoke coolly as the man screamed in despair.

Daniel's screech shot ice through Ariel's veins, as horrified gasps filled the air around her. The smell of his burning flesh wafted over the crowd and the clanging of metal against metal pounded, as his body convulsed violently. When the guard stepped away, retrieving the rod, Daniel's torso was marked. His flesh had peeled away, exposing his bloody, charred flesh beneath. He had soiled himself and the mixture of aromas nauseated the crowd, who stood frozen. Horrified faces, among deadpan expression of those who had seen it all before. The marked man whimpered, tears streaking his contorted face as he hung limply by the chains, blood streaking, reaching out to the wooden floor.

"Justice has been carried out. Daniel, son of Annabelle, from this day forward you will not carry your mother's name and be known only as Daniel. You shall seed no more vessels, nor be A Watcher. May your islander brothers treat you with the same kindness you have treated our guest." She pursed her mouth in contempt and looked to Eric whose deadpan face did not flinch.

"Take him away, clean him up." Eric's voice held tenderness that Ariel did not expect.

When the man was removed from the stage, Tay stepped forward once more. "Bring them."

Four guardsmen ushered three naked women onto the stage. They huddled together as if they could find safety within one another.

"Step fourth Hattie, daughter of Iris, Jane, daughter of Maria and Lila, daughter of Vera." Tay addressed the crowd.

"These young vessels are yet to find a mate. Though our island is teeming with strong, virile specimen, these vessels are yet to give themselves away. They have not fulfilled their duty and will now be taken as per our law."

Once again Tay looked to Eric, who nodded at the guardsmen, his face twisted in a grimace. The three women shrieked as they were pried apart. Trying to cover themselves up, they began whimpering and begging, just as Daniel had done. "No, please, don't do this."

"Your mates have been chosen for you. Your duty will be fulfilled."

"No!" the women begged as three masked, naked men climbed the stage. They were all marked with the symbol of the guard. It would be the only time in their lives that they would be allowed to touch a woman.

The women were forced onto their backs. They wriggled and bucked as they were held down then mounted. Shrieks of terror and despair escaped them as the men took them. Ariel looked away, pressing her head into Ben's chest, which rose and fell in heavy uneven breaths.

The taken women's shrieks fell away, and all that was left was soft sobbing and the groans and grunts of the men as they fulfilled their duty. Ariel felt eyes on the back on her neck and scanned the stage. The Watcher Tay had her eyes anchored on Ariel, the look intense and disturbing. Ariel looked away, a cold chill filled her body. Her chest felt as if it might explode. She grabbed onto Ben, steadying herself.

The groans died down as each guard finished. They rose and left the women on the floor and retreated off the stage. Tay looked to the female Watchers behind her. "Take them, clean them, welcome them into the fold of womanhood." She smiled serenely as she said the last.

The Watchers peeled the taken women from the hard, wooden floors. Their tear-streaked faces shell-shocked as they sucked in breath, their bodies limp as they struggled to walk, their unstable steps assisted by the older women.

Tay stepped forward and scanned the crowds. "Do not mourn for those who have been judged today, for their paths had been chosen by their actions alone. Stock must be taken, action witnessed by all." Her unnatural grin graced her face once more. "A feast shall await you all tonight as a farewell. We thank you for performing your duties and look forward to hosting you once more. You have seven hours left to enjoy one another on our shores. Do so at your pleasure. All duties have been fulfilled."

A subdued murmur rose as the crowd began to disperse. The Watchers descended the platform, somehow melting into the island, remaining unseen but always watching.

When Ben and Ariel retreated to what Ariel hoped was a safe distance, she pushed away from Ben and ran to the tree line, her body heaving violently..

Ben was behind her, drawing her hair away from her face.

Ariel wiped her mouth, certain that her body was done, and gave him a distressed look.

"That could have been us," she whispered harshly.

"But it wasn't," Ben pulled her to him and whispered in her ear as he kissed her sweaty forehead.

"But…"

"It wasn't…"

"They know…" Her voice held the icy shards of fear.

"If they knew, we would not be here." He tucked an errant hair behind her ear.

Still shaking, she sat in his arms until tears trickled down her face. She sobbed into his chest, her hands clutching at his flesh as if willing him to take her pain. Ben's silence soothed only by his slow rocking and the comforting feel of his hands on her back.

They did not join the feast. Cries of merriment and singing rose from the mess hall. They sat on the beach, the waves lapped at her feet as they took in the last rays of the sun.

"I don't want to say goodbye again." Her voice was hoarse and uneasy.

"Pretty sure we have no choice."

"Why is this so much harder than it was five years ago?"

"Maybe it's because you finally love me, too?"

"I have always loved you, you fool."

His eyes grew large and he found her mouth, swallowing her words.

When he broke away from her, his lips glistened and his heart raced. "It's only three months," he breathed.

"They will feel longer than the last five years."

"But then we will be together again." His eyes found hers swollen with tears.

"Till then, my love." She bit her lip, her face forlorn.

"Till then."

They embraced, and he held her as if he was about to break and she was the glue that was keeping him in one piece. His lips on hers like words that didn't need to be spoken.

14

HOME

"You're back." Rosalie held her arm open, excited to see her younger sister. Ariel embraced her, delighted to see her sister smile. Mama Beth wedged herself between the sisters, pushing them apart and looked Ariel, up and down.

"Did you make me a beautiful grandchild?" She didn't mince her words.

"Mom." Ariel's eyes widened as she waved her mother off.

"Good." Mama Beth chuckled. "I hope you tried enough times with enough men to make sure."

Ariel said nothing as Rosalie slipped an arm around her shoulder and pulled her close as they walked home.

"So, was Ben there?" Rosalie whispered.

"He was." Ariel's heart leapt at the mention of his name and she wrung her wrists.

Rosalie screeched in delight, making assumptions Ariel did not deny.

Once home, her mother offered to make her a bath. She nodded in thanks and waited for the bath water to fill the tub.

Ariel peeled off her stained white dress, his mark and smell a fresh reminder of all they hadn't done. She sank into the hot water, wishing to wash away the hurt and pain of the last seven days. She allowed delight to soak into her bones in their stead. Her body tingled as she thought of Ben, his kiss, his burning touch. Her heart ached, knowing all that she could never have.

When she had toweled herself off, she found her mother and sister eagerly awaiting outside the bathroom door. Ariel gave them an apologetic look, explaining she was too tired to talk, much to her mother's delight. Ariel went to her room, closing the door behind her. For a short moment, she leaned against the wooden barrier and exhaled.

Tying her hair up, she slipped into a singlet and shorts. The sensation of clothes on her body a comfort. No one to peek at her body through transparent fabric. No one to measure or judge or flirt or assume. She had never found so much freedom in clothing. Her singlet clung to her in a safe embrace and she relished the sensation as she lay on her bed missing Ben's voice, his arms, the feel of his hair beneath her fingers, wondering how he was faring.

As the days passed, her mother's insistent questions and harassment took their toll. Ariel once again asked Mama Beth for extra chores. Work helped her avoid her mother, but more importantly, it helped time move during the days where her mind kept wandering back to Ishmin.

When the red flood begun between her legs, her mother's disapproving side glances and sour looks did not go unnoticed.

For twelve long weeks, she was given no reprieve. The constant tirade of interrogation did not stop with Mama Beth. Rosalie and Mia pestered her for details since her return, and avoiding them wasn't as easy.

Ariel didn't know how to answer their questions. In part because she didn't have the answers they were looking for and also because she didn't want to admit some of the answers to herself.

When they asked about their reunion, she turned red and shook her head. The girls shrieked, interpreting her embarrassment in their own ways. She could never tell a soul the real events of that night. When they asked how he was, all she could say was gentle. They both grinned a devilish grin that Ariel didn't quite understand the meaning of. When they asked if he was all that she was hoping for, she wanted to tell them that he was so much more but cut them off with assurances that they were nothing more than friends. Friends who had done their duty. Despite her best efforts to hide behind endless jobs and short answers, they were never satisfied.

Ariel knew her friend well. Though she loved to pry, she loved nothing more than talking about herself and so when her questions became unnerving, Ariel would often ask her the very same questions and Mia would get lost in her answers, sparing her friend no details. Sharing a full and explicit account of her mating exploits.

Mia enjoyed five mates. All of whom had taken her in various ways which Mia happily demonstrated. Ariel looked away. The thought of Ben doing any of those things to her made her face burn and her body tingle with fear while aching with desire.

Mia was with child. By the twelfth week, Mia's flat belly had begun to swell. Her bosom had doubled in size and Ariel would often see her cradling the tiny bump like she would the baby within. Mia's initial tiredness had passed, and she was excited to send her friend back into Ben's arms. Although she had encouraged her numerous times to consider making other 'friends' she could mate with.

Ariel knew her friend was only trying to be helpful, she had become withdrawn. Mia and Rosalie had put it down to disappointment. They had both come back with child after their first visit to Ishmin.

At the siren on her 13th week she stood on the beach once more, her body poked and checked, cleansed and adorned.

She felt as if a swarm of hummingbirds had taken flight inside her chest and were threatening to burst through. She ground her teeth as her mother ensured to remind her of her duty. Mama Beth insisted of more frequent activity and with a larger number of mates. She wished her daughter well and demanded Ariel come back with her grandchild.

Ariel gave her mother a wan smile, knowing that if Ben would keep his promise Mama Beth would once again be disappointed. Her departure was hasty as she boarded the boat and did not look back.

As Ishmin came into view, Ariel's stomach was in knots. She was unsure if it was the gentle rocking of the boat on the waves or the anticipation of seeing Ben once more.

15

SECOND MEETING

S he slouched as she stood in line. Another line where she would be recorded, examined and placed into a tent. She was beginning to feel like a sheep in a herd. At least this line didn't lead to the slaughterhouse. Not yet, she added to herself as memories of her last day on Ishmin surfaced. She pushed the thought away as she gave a chagrined smile to the woman who studied her through grey eyes encircled by radiating deep lines. Her dark hair tigered by strands of white. Loose skin hung from her thin arms.

Ariel was shown to her tent. Still blue. She sat on the bed, taking a few deep breaths to calm herself. She waited for the music to grow, for the bubble of noise to rise until it exploded over the island, the throbbing beat pulsating like a heartbeat.

Ariel gathered herself and made her way to the meeting area.

She scanned the bar. Men and women clad in the traditional whites were scattered along the wooden structure, alcohol exchanging hands, tongues in wild dances. She didn't see Ben.

She searched the dance floor, where flesh met flesh in raw

undulating movements. The dance floor was as fluid as the ocean they had all come from. Faces drawn in glee and desire moved wildly. And yet he wasn't there.

Ariel bit her lip, shifting her weight.

"Didn't think I'd be seeing you again so soon." The familiar voice crawled up her skin.

"Still not interested, Liam." Her voice was dry.

"And why not?" He had come to stand by her, his hand hovering just above her buttocks, threatening to travel down. "If we mate, you won't be back for a year, and when you do return, you'll be wanting only me again."

She stepped away from his touch and turned to face him. "Is that so?"

"Oh, yes." He stepped toward her, closing the gap.

"Well, then, if that's true, why are you chasing me and not being chased by all these women which you say can't get enough of you? Surely they can't all be with child?"

"Well – "

"Yes, well, maybe you are not as good a mate as you proclaim yourself to be."

"I – "

"You know, girls talk. A lot. Do you ever wonder if your name has come up?"

"With you around, Ariel, that's not the only thing that comes up." He wiggled his hips and gyrated madly, ensuring she understood.

Ariel grimaced and shot a darting gaze to the dance floor. Still no Ben.

"Why can you not take no for an answer like everyone else? They all walked away, they all moved on."

"Why do you insist on playing hard to get?" He pushed Ariel onto the wall, his groin pushing against her body

"Liam," she started, "if you do not get away from me now, the next kick I give you will ensure you will never mate again, because there's no way you will be getting that thing up ever again."

Liam froze and looked into her eyes. Lust turned into rage.

"I *will* have you looking up at me one day." Liam scowled at her.

"That will *never* happen."

"Am I interrupting something?"

"No." Ariel's voice didn't waver as she ducked under Liam's arm and rushed to Ben.

Ben's face exploded in a delighted smile as Ariel's body fell against his, her soft lips tenderly meeting his for a second.

"Hi." She gave him a wide smile.

"Hi." He returned the gesture.

"I see," growled Liam as he pushed by them, ensuring his shoulder struck Ben's chest. "Ben." He said with acid in his voice.

"Liam." Ben smirked at the man whose wounded ego saw him walking straight to the bar.

"How long were you standing there?"

"Long enough to see you hadn't changed your mind about me."

"So, you saw him harassing me?" Her eyes narrowed.

"Yes."

"And you didn't come to rescue me?"

"I'm pretty sure you made it clear last time, you were in no need of rescue. And after seeing what you did to that man last time you saw him, I was taking no chances." He covered his groin and stepped back from her.

She giggled and elbowed him playfully. "I don't *need* to be rescued, but it would have been nice, anyway."

"Didn't want to take any chances…"

"Oh, shut up already."

"Make me."

Ariel pushed herself on her tiptoes, slamming her lips into his. She could feel his entire body responding to her. The momentary stillness of the muscles, the intake of breath, and then he melted into her, his tongue dancing widely with hers, his strong arms wrapped around her, pulling her closer as if he wanted to be a part of her.

They broke apart.

"I thought you weren't here." She looked at him, wide eyes grabbing at his flesh.

"Nothing will keep me away from you." He pulled her closer. "Would you like to get out of here?" his husky voice breathed into her ear.

"I thought we had a deal."

"We do, but I haven't seen you in three months and I want you all to myself, just for a while."

Ariel smiled at his candour, at his tenderness and slid her hand into his, leading him away from the chaos and noise and towards the quieter beach.

They walked in silence until she felt the cool water licking at her toes.

"How did your mom take it?"

"Not good." Ariel sighed. "She doesn't hide disappointment well."

Ben nodded, a grin splitting his face. "I remember. What about Rosalie?"

"I think she suspects the way I feel, but I haven't said a thing. My mom thinks I need to take on other mates."

"Does she now?" His head cocked slightly, eyebrows rising.

"She seems to think the one that I have chosen is not alpha enough or I would have been back with her grandchild."

"Is that right?" His eyebrows rose further.

"She seems to think that I need to do *it* more often, with more men," she chided as he got more agitated.

Without warning, she felt her legs get swept from beneath her. Ben caught her when she fell into the sand. He was on top of her, pinning her down on the sand, his eyes blazing.

Without hesitation, he kissed her, hard, his lips devouring hers, his hunger insatiable. His restless arms scouring her body, his fingers digging into hidden flesh.

"Hey." She took his face in her hands and looked into his eyes. "I was only joking."

"I know." He was breathless as he loosened his grip. "I just don't ever want to think about that."

He buried himself in her neck, her flesh breaking out in goosebumps as his lips left a gentle heat trail on her skin. His hand travelled up to the clasp behind her neck and he stopped, his eyes looking at her questioningly.

Ariel nodded in answer, her grip tightening against his back. With clumsy fingers, he grabbed at the plastic ring and unclipped her dress, the fabric falling around her shoulders. His lips left hers, traveling to her jaw, peppering a trail of kisses to her neck and shoulders. He looked at her once more, asking for permission which came back in the form of silence.

Tugging on the dress, he teased the fabric from her body, revealing her bosom. Her chest heaved and her breasts bulged, no longer the flat-chested girl he remembered. Her flesh was swollen and white, the pink nipples hard and splendid.

He gasped at the sight of her.

At that, Ariel bucked and pushed him off her, a hand flew to her breasts providing cover. "Stop."

"Ariel, I –"He ran a hand through his hair. "You're just so beautiful. I'm sorry, I didn't mean to – "

She swallowed his apology with a soft, tender kiss, her bare chest pressed against his. "I know, I'm just... not ready, not yet... I'm sorry." She cast her eyes down a flush crept across her cheeks.

Ben nodded, his lip pressed in a tight line. "Should we..." he cleared his throat, "finish the show?" His warm whisper sent shivers down her spine.

She clenched her jaw, nodding, and allowed him to his relief.

When it was done, he reached for the folds of her dress and reset the clasp then fell back into the sand.

"I'm sorry." She covered her face in her hands, her knees pulled tightly to her caved chest.

"Don't be." His voice almost a whisper as he tried to regain his senses. "Take all the time you need." He exhaled deeply.

Her silence the only response.

"Come lie with me. Please." He waited, until slowly, she began to uncurl allowing her frigid body to melt and tangle in his. They watched the stars as the earth stopped spinning.

"I need to go clean up. This stain will show in the morning." She rose to her feet.

"Do you need help?"

"Think you've helped enough." She winked at him and left him where he lay.

The shower cubicle protruded from between the tents like a white whale in a blue sea. The looming rectangular building was well lit and she weaved her way to it, holding the sticky dress away from her body.

Ariel stepped in, her feet sinking into the moist sand. She reached for the sink, a bucket of steaming water by her feet. She heard the faint whimper. She froze. The muted sobbing came from behind a wall, and she rounded it slowly.

She saw the woman slouched on the ground, her shaking body leaning against the wall, her dress stained with a thin trail of blood. The woman held her breath as she saw Ariel, terror in her eyes.

"It's okay," Ariel whispered to her and made to move closer. The woman flinched, sucking in breath.

Ariel stepped closer and slid along the wall until she was side by side with the woman.

Gliding her hands around her trembling shoulders, Ariel pulled the woman close and rocked her.

"Shhh, you're okay now."

She waited until the other woman calmed.

"What's your name?"

"Hannah."

"I'm Ariel. What happened to you? Would you like me to call a Watcher?"

"No! Don't do that." She groped Ariel's hand, her eyes wide, her nostrils flaring.

"Okay, no Watchers. What happened? Who hurt you?"

"It was my fault. I said he could. He seemed nice, but then he was so rough and I cried and I asked him to stop, but we had already started. I didn't think it would hurt; he promised it wouldn't…" she spurted and shifted.

"It's okay, you're safe now."

"I don't want to do it again. I'm scared. What if it hurts again?" She shivered under Ariel.

Hannah looked to Ariel, her bloodshot eyes swollen with tears. "Did it hurt your first time, too? Will it always hurt?"

Ariel bit her lip, squeezing the girl's shoulder. "No, it doesn't always hurt." Her heart thumped in her ears as she heard the words spill from her mouth, her eyes landing on the red stain.

"Maybe I won't have to do it again. I don't want to."

"You don't have to."

"But what if I didn't get all his seed? I'd have to come back in three months," she cried, fresh tears carving her features.

"They are not all like that."

"They aren't?"

"No. Some are gentle, caring."

"Do you know any? Can you show me?"

Ariel cleared her throat. "It will be better tomorrow. Let me help you clean up."

Ariel helped Hannah to her feet. Ariel dipped a clean cloth in the bucket and wiped her face, her tears vanishing under a sheen of water. She unclasped the woman's dress and it fell to the floor like a rag. Ariel sank a cloth into the warm bucket and rung off the excess water. The warm cloth glided with ease along Hannah's bruised body. She winced as Ariel trailed the red marks along her back and abdomen, wiping away the fear and hurt.

Ariel wrung out the cloth once more, her hand shivered as she clenched her jaw, holding her feelings at bay. She handed Hannah the wet cloth, allowing her to wipe the bloody trail herself, grimacing as the heated rag touched the apex of her legs. When she was clean, Ariel helped her stand and slip back into her tainted dress.

"Let me take you to your tent," she offered and Hannah nodded her thanks

"I'm in number 47."

Ariel steered her to her tent and set her gently onto her cot. She curled up as Ariel covered her with a thin sheet.

"Thank you," Hannah offered when Ariel turned to leave. She grabbed her arm. "I'm scared."

Ariel twisted her wrists from the woman's grip and stroked her head. "It will be better tomorrow," she assured her, waiting for her to fall asleep.

Ariel slipped out of the tent, terror seizing her heart.

They had put on another show, her body reacting to his more fiercely than she had anticipated, yet her mind remained seized with terror. He lay by her side panting, the warmth of him fading from her body as it cooled into a sticky pool.

"It wasn't always like this," she said, breaking her silence.

"What?"

"The way we live, Mating Season."

"Wasn't it?" He tilted his head toward her.

"No, there was a time when there was a thing called marriage."

"I've never heard that term before. Is it a good thing?"

"I don't know, but I think it's better than this." His hand tightened around her.

"What is it, then? This Marriage?"

"I read about it in a book I found once. I asked my mom about it and she said it was a myth."

"But what is it?"

"It's a promise."

"Of what?"

"It's a promise people used to make to one another, sometimes even before they had kids." She lifted off his chest and turned to look into his eyes. "They promised to stay together and raise their children together. They would share a house, share chores, and share the child-rearing."

She watched as Ben's eyes grew wider.

"They promised to be with only one another, not other mates." She bit her lip before saying the last. "They promised to love one another until death."

Ben stayed silent, mulling over all she had said.

"Where is this book, Ariel?"

"My mother burned it when I questioned her about it. Don't you remember?"

Ben stared up at the dark sky, his fingers absently tracing the lines of Ariel's back.

"So, there was a time that people stayed together? All the time?"

"Yes."

"And they, a man and a woman, would raise children? Together? Watch them grow? On the same island?"

"Yes. But there were no islands then." Ben shook his head at her words. She could feel his heart pounding under her.

He pushed himself off the sand and turned to look at her. "Is that something you would want to do? With me?" She could hear the hesitation in his voice, the uncertainty.

"More than anything in the world." She gave him a wan smile and her eyes dropped from his. "But I don't think we will ever be allowed to. You know what the rules are. You know what the living arrangements are. How are we going to be able to do this?"

"There has to be a way."

"How?"

"I don't know, but I have to believe that there will come a time when we can be together. There has to be a way where I don't have to wait three months just to see you for a week. There has to be a way where I don't have to wait that long to be able to feel your body underneath me, to be able to feel your warmth, your lips, your touch."

His words fell away.

Ariel pulled away from his body and sat up, looking at the ocean. "I want to believe that, too. That there could be a way for us, but I just don't see it happening."

"We can run away, go away. Just float around the ocean until we find our own island."

"And if we don't find an island?"

"Then we'll be on a boat, together."

She snorted at the idea. They both knew he was grasping at straws.

"Okay, so let's say that somehow I will let you talk me into your boat. What about our families? Rosalie? Her boys?"

"Mama Beth?"

"We can leave her behind," Ariel chided.

Ben's body deflated as he reached for her. "I don't have a family, not really, but if you come with me, we can make a new kind of family, one where we have a child and he can enjoy both of us, his entire life. Our entire lives."

"He?"

"Or she…"

"Ben…" She gave him a pained look. "Don't do this…"

"We could. Just you and me and them." He clenched his jaw as he clutched at her arm.

"I don't want to live on your imaginary boat! Why have kids deprived of knowing their grandmother and aunt and nephews? You didn't get to have a family, so having gone through that, why would you want to deny your future children a chance of being raised by those who love them?"

"But I would love them. If only I'd be given a chance."

"Ben."

"No! Why should that child be robbed of the opportunity of loving me? Why can't they have a father and a mother? Why should I lose at every possible turn?"

She saw him, breakable and vulnerable, a child himself seeking love and shelter, seeking the warmth he had been deprived of the day he was torn from his home. He was right. This was no way to raise children. How could she have been so blind?

Ariel wrapped her arms around him, his head falling onto her shoulders. As she rocked him, his hot tears spilt down her back, leaving rivulets of pain and despair.

"What if we just ask?" Her soft voice pierced through his anguish.

"Ask?" He raised his head, looking at her, his eyes shining with tears.

"Yes. What if we ask? We can go to The Watchers, tell them that we want to be together, stay together. They cannot keep us apart. I won't let them keep me away from you forever." She stroked his face.

"That's madness, Ariel. You know what they could do to us."

She ground her teeth, deep in thought. "What about my mom? Let me talk to my mom first. Let me see what she says. Maybe she will help."

"Mama Beth? Help us?" She heard the snigger in his voice.

"I think you underestimate what my mother is willing to do for her daughter, and for her grandchild, born or unborn."

"Ariel, what if she reports us?"

"It's a risk we must take."

"I can't watch you be taken by another."

"She won't let it come to that."

"But – "

Her lips landed on his, delicate and sweet, pulling away the last edges of doubt and fear.

"I won't let it come to that," she whispered as she fell into his longing, fierce embrace. Their lips locked in desperation, she fell to the soft sand beneath him, despair giving way to desire. Seeking comfort in her body.

"And tell your mom, there will be no other men, not ever."

"Yes, sir."

"Oh, I like the sound of that." They giggled.

"Well, don't get used to it." She winked at him.

He rolled off her, and Ariel placed her head on his chest. She could hear his heartbeat. And noticed the bulge in his pants.

"You seem to have a tent peg problem."

He looked down as if confirming, "That I do. Would you like to help me with that?"

"I'm still enduring the joy of the last time I helped you

with that…" She grimaced at her moist dress. "Just make sure you keep that thing away from me."

He exaggerated a sigh and flashed her a set of white teeth, then let his head fall back into his hand.

When the siren came on the seventh day, she unglued herself from him in silence. Any spoken words would be wasted and last goodbyes crushing. They had endured The Taking of another, they had held onto hope.

She boarded the boat once more, grief clawing its dark tentacles into her. She has lost him again, if only for a short time. His touch lingered long after the lights of the island were no longer visible.

16

MAMA BETH

"What's wrong with you child? You should be practically dancing around."

Ariel shuffled into the kitchen, sidestepping a sticky spot on the floor her mother no doubt left for her to clean. She opened the fridge and, finding nothing to soothe the cramping in her belly, shut it once more.

"No appetite?" Her mother raised a brow.

"Just tired."

"You should also be hungry."

Ariel rolled her eyes, "Mama, why do we live like this?"

"You know why."

"Tell me again."

The older woman studied her daughter's face and stepped back into the kitchen, pulling a chair and plopping into it.

"What's going on, Ariel?"

"Tell me."

The older woman sighed. "In the beginning there was one land. All of humanity lived together. For some, this was merriment, but for the majority this meant fear and devastation. Men ruled the earth, and with their rule came tyranny and violence. Rape and pillaging, murder and wars. The last of the great wars ended the world. Greed and lust brought such hatred that, with the great war, came a great explosion. It tore the earth itself into islands. Those who were left understood the way to peace. There must be segregation of the sexes, for lust leads to violence and greed, to rape and conquers. With sex no longer a weapon, peace fell, and the broken population was able to reawaken. Women, fertile vessels, were sent to claim the seed of men who were powerless to possess them. Women held, and continue to hold all the power. They may consent or forbid mating. Women will produce with the best specimen and grow children. They will nurture and love and will raise good men. Men who no longer seek to claim but to love, provide, and nurture. They hold desires and give pleasure without pain."

She exhaled deeply as she finished her monologue, Ariel deep in thought. "How long ago did this happen?"

"Three hundred years." Mama Beth pulled out her little tobacco box and began expertly rolling a cigarette, sprinkling the dried tobacco on the white paper and rolling it in between calloused dry fingers. She licked the edge of the paper and stuck it shut. Admiring her handiwork, she put the cigarette to her mouth and lit it taking a long drag.

"And there have been reports of the water levels dropping, of new-found lands?"

"What is this about, Ariel?" She narrowed her eyes studying her daughter.

"Can men change their ways?"

"They have." She blew out a long trail of white smoke.

"So can we change the way we live?"

"Men may have changed, but not their nature. That will never change."

"I don't understand." As the words left her mouth, she thought of that day when the ball had hit her face on the beach, Ben's puffed chest and battle-ready face.

Her mother took another long drag and shifted in her

chair. She blew perfect white smoke rings, which disintegrated as the breeze carried them away. "Men have changed because they have been kept deprived of the things that drive them to war. They are deprived of power, they are deprived of space, they are deprived of lust."

"Does being deprived not drive them to try and claim these things?"

Mama Beth shook her head. "Indeed. But they are given all these things willingly at short, predictable intervals, so that their deprivation does not grow beyond the boundaries of what is natural." She stood up and paced around the room. "They are given power when they possess our bodies, for they believe that they are in control, and their lust and desires are fed. They do not need to seek them, for everyone mates. Everyone is satisfied."

"And space?"

"They have space on their islands, and if they do not have enough, they take it from one another. We may be peaceful, but men still find reasons to battle."

"You said that we nurture and grow thoughtful, calm men. So why over four generations have men not changed?"

"Because, my dear Ariel, they are also deprived of love." At that they both fell silent, smoke filling the air as Mama Beth dragged and blew from her roll-up.

"So why can't we change?"

Mama Beth shrugged. "Humanity doesn't change. We can go back to the old days, but soon chaos will reign once again."

"But what if men and women lived together? What if there was love?"

"Ha!" Mama Beth smirked. "You mean happily ever afters?"

Ariel frowned at the response.

"Trust me, my dear, there is no such thing, and who ever filled your head with such notions should be thrown out to sea. Men don't love, they lust. They don't stick around, they stray. Why milk the same cow when you can get milk from all the cows? Men do not want to raise children or comfort sadness. They are not tender. They are brutes which hold one purpose only, and if you give them any power, they will wield it and twist it and there will be no coming back from it."

Ariel sat in stunned silence as her mother finished her tirade.

"They are not all like that."

Mama Beth raised her eyebrows.

"Ben is not like that. Mama Cath raised him well."

"I do not doubt Cath, but I do recall a certain boy asking to see what lay beneath your clothes, and how crushed you were when what you had was not to his pleasure."

"How do you know about that?" Ariel shot from her chair, recoiling from the table.

"There is little on this Island I do not know."

"It was a long time ago. We were only kids. People change."

"They don't."

"I love him." She blurted the words out as if they were a disease.

Mama Beth said nothing, dragging slowly on her roll-up and nodding her head.

"Mama – "

"I heard you." Her voice was cool as she blew perfect smoke rings. "You think he feels the same?"

"I know he does."

Mama Beth smirked. "What promises did he make when he was inside you? None will come true."

Ariel bit her tongue at the remark. Her mother didn't know.

"I need your help."

"No."

"Please."

Mama Beth stood up, stamping the cigarette out in the ashtray. "Whatever feelings you think you have, you must forget them. Find another mate and move on. Do not get attached. You and Ben can never be more than what you already are."

"But with your help, we could – "

"No! You cannot. I will not allow it. Your silly childhood crush has gone on for too long and has clouded your judgment. If you did not fall pregnant on this round, I will make sure The Watchers pick another for you."

"You can't do that. That's against the rules."

"There are always exceptions."

"So why won't you make one for me?"

"Because what you ask will end in disaster."

"How can it? We love each other. What more is there?"

"There is heartbreak. Heartbreak which I will have to glue together when you are in pieces."

"You've never wanted me to be happy," Ariel shouted at her mother as her eyes welled with tears.

"That's all we've ever wanted for you." Mama Beth reached for her daughter, who flinched away, sidestepping her.

"Liar." It was a sharp, shrill accusation.

"Ariel, wait!" Mama Beth shouted after her as Ariel flew out of the house and ran down the path.

"I thought I might find you here." Mama Beth sat next to her daughter on the rock. "You always come here when you are upset."

Ariel remained silent, seething in her anger. She watched the waves break against the hard stone, white spittle flying in the air and falling on to her feet in an angry dance.

"I have always loved you, Ariel." Ariel remained motionless. "Almost more than I loved your father." At that Ariel shifted and turned to her mother, her mouth falling open, her body growing stiff.

"There you go, looking at me through his eyes." Mama Beth stroked Ariel's cheek and let her hand drop.

"He was so handsome, tall and broad. You have his eyes and nose. Sometimes when you move, I can see him in you, your mannerisms." Her eyes glazed over. "He promised me so many things, Ariel." She smiled a bitter, sad smile. "We gave one another our everything. I gave him my heart."

She pursed her lips and a single tear fell from her eye. "We were going to change the world. We were going to be the ones who made it. Instead there were only broken promises and broken hearts and so much loneliness and grief." She wiped her cheek, her face growing stern once more. "Can't you see, child, we are only trying to protect you?"

"We?"

"Me." Mama Beth cleared her throat, shifting on the rock.

"Ben will never hurt me, Mama."

"Not intentionally." Mama Beth stroked Ariel's hair.

"Not ever."

"You can't know that."

"But I do.'

"How, sweet child?"

Ariel remained silent. She could not reveal the truth, not even to her mother.

Mama Beth sighed and placed her hand on her daughter's. "Love?"

"We want to be together, till death do us part."

"You want to make promises to one another?"

"Yes."

She nodded and studied her daughter's face, smiling

briefly at her young features. "I will do what I can for you, but don't say I didn't warn you when the time comes."

Ariel squealed and wrapped her hands around her mother, toppling them over. "Thank you, Mama."

The older woman recovered and pushed away from her daughter standing up. "And Ariel?"

"Yes Mama?"

"You won't be able to keep fooling The Watchers. You must do what you are designed to do. Love might not keep you two together, but the power of a child might."

With that, Mama Beth spun and walked away, leaving Ariel's mouth gaping and heart racing.

The afternoon breeze swept across Inan when Ariel returned home. Despite wanting nothing more but to know how much Mama Beth actually knew, Ariel kept her mouth shut as she entered her home. The sitting area was veiled in a blue-white cloud. Her mother's figure swallowed by the wisps of curling smoke as she blew out another perfect circle into the thick haze. Mama Beth grunted in greeting and put out the smouldering butt in the overflowing ashtray.

"Mama?"

"Come here, Ariel."

Ariel pushed through the blanket of smoke and went to her mother, who had produced a pencil and a ripped piece of paper smaller than her thumb.

She leaned down into her ear and whispered in a hoarse, dry voice, "Would you like to send him a message?"

Ariel's hand shot to her mouth and she studied her mother through large eyes, trying to find words which wouldn't form.

"Well?" Her mother's hot breath was at her ear.

"Yes, but how?"

"Everyone has a price."

"And what would be the price of this?" Ariel stepped back, searching her mother's face.

"Don't worry yourself with petty details. Just write." She grabbed her daughter's wrist. "No names, not long, something that will tell him it's from you."

Ariel nodded and brought the pencil to her lips, biting on the wood. The taste of cold lead seeped into her mouth as a small smile spread across her face.

I told you so.

She handed the shredded paper to her mother, who studied it. "This?"

Ariel nodded, chewing on the inside of her cheek.

Mama Beth grunted, once more folding the paper into an impossibly small white shard and tucking it into her bra. Without another word she left the house, leaving Ariel engulfed in silence and smoke.

1 7

TEST

For a fifth day, Ariel's head burned with fever as she tried to push her weak body from the bed.

"You can't go, Ariel. You can't even stand." Mama Beth's stern face looked at her from above.

"I have to go see him. If I don't…." The possibility stabbed at her heart like daggers.

"You can't think of that right now."

"It's all I can think about, Mama. If he is summoned and I am not, he will be forced to…"

"Forced?" Mama Beth couldn't suppress her smirk.

Ariel moaned with pain as she tried to push herself off the bed, falling with a thud to the floor. "Help me." Tears ran down her face, her weak body fighting the disease.

Her mother stepped closer and lifted her daughter, placing her back on the bed. Brushing the hair from her eyes, she soothed the sick child. "All will be as it is meant to be."

"Please, let me go," Ariel croaked through tears and sickness.

"I will, darling. Just get some rest."

W hen Ariel opened her eyes once more, harsh sunlight bathed her room. Her body still felt weak, but she was able to push herself up.

She reached for the glass of water which had been left by her bed. It tasted hot and stale, as if it had been sitting there for a while.

When she thought she could, Ariel stood up and shuffled to the kitchen. She found Mama Beth on the couch. She raised an eyebrow in greeting as if surprised to see her walking around.

"What day is it?" Her voice throaty and scratched.

"Sunday." Mama Beth's deadpan expression greeted Ariel as her face contorted in a new kind of pain.

"I've missed it." Her small body, still weak, crumpled to the ground. "Where is Rosalie?"

"She's gone." Mama Beth's voice was calm and even.

Ariel looked at her mother through bloodshot eyes. "Where?"

Mama Beth remained silent.

"Where?" Her eyes narrowed to slits.

"Ishmin."

"What?" Ariel's sobs turned to rage.

"She has gone in your stead." Still calm, she sat watching her daughter writhe on the floor.

"What have you done? You knew she didn't ever want to go back. What did you do?" Ariel's shrill scream penetrated her mother's steel resolve.

Mama Beth rose from the couch and came to stand over her daughter. "One day you will learn that sometimes we do what we must and not what we want."

"What are you saying?"

"Ariel…"

"She wouldn't, we talked, she would never, he won't…" White rage took hold of Ariel. Her entire body shook with the purity of it as its tentacles crawled behind her eyes and through her body.

"No!" she screamed. "No, no, no, no, no!" The sheer surge of anger that consumed her needed an escape. Her body was burning from the inside and she felt as if she may explode.

"Ariel…" But she no longer heard her mother's voice.

"No!" she screamed once more as she ran through the door and down the path. She sprinted to the beach, her nightgown sticking to her body, the fabric floating behind her like a ghost.

The sea water splashed and parted as she hurtled into it, diving in a frenzy, crashing and pushing against the waves. Her usual perfect strokes, sloppy and angry, didn't gain much ground against the rising tide. The usually gentle, welcoming sea now like a wall, putting up barrier after barrier, pushing back her advances.

As her strength dwindled, as did her anger. The salty water like a balm to the open wound, seething just below the surface. Ariel punched at the water and screamed for Rosalie, for Ben, for the universe, but no answers came. Depleted and defeated, she floated on the surface, allowing the current to sweep her away and wash her back to shore where she lay like a dying fish.

When Mama Beth came to find her, her flesh was pink from the hot sun and her lips dry, her body in need of quenching. She helped her daughter back to the house, where she bathed and dried her, quenched her thirst and placated her quivering body as she fell asleep once more in a flood of tears.

The fever had broken overnight and her body felt warmth, the shivering subsided. She dreamt of being held. Of a strong body attached to hers, of salt and sand in her bed.

She concentrated on her dream, not wanting the sensation to fade. A bare chest against her back, light breath on her neck and heavy arms around her waist.

She heard the grunt as she stirred and her body froze.

Her hand found the ones wrapped around her, and long fingers closed around hers.

She shifted, spun, and was looking into Ben's face.

He smiled at her dreamily.

"I'm dreaming," she said, her voice sleepy.

"No, you're not."

"I have to be, because you can't be real. You can't be here, in my bed."

"But I am."

"Stop."

"Can a dream do this?" He brushed a lock of hair away from her cheek and placed a delicate peck on the exposed skin, still warm from her pillow.

Her eyes grew wider as they searched his face. Her hands reached for him, stabbing at his flesh.

"Ben? How?"

He cut her off with a finger to her lips as her voice screeched in the silent house.

Bolting up, she pulled at the sheet, covering her body. She glared at his naked torso. "What are you doing here? How did you get here? What's going on?"

"I told you so..."

"I told you so?" Her face crinkled and she hitched one brow. "You got my note?"

He nodded, grinning.

"So, does that mean that Mama is..."

"Slow down, Ariel. Is this the way you always say good morning?" He flashed her a toothy grin and pulled her arm from beneath her, her body collapsing onto his. Ben kissed her, a soft, tender kiss.

"Hi." He smiled softly at her.

"Hi." She stroked his face, the creases deepening. "How are you here?"

"Rosalie came to get me."

"Rosalie? Did you see her? Did you…" She swallowed, the words a lump in her throat.

"No! I mean, yes, I saw her, but no, we didn't. I wouldn't." He flinched at her unsaid accusation.

"I know what you said, but there are rules."

"And yet here we are." He hitched an eyebrow as if it was a challenge.

"How are you here?" She repeated the question.

"Rosalie came to get me."

"Get you?"

His expression turned dark as his grip tightened around her. "You didn't show. I waited for hours and you didn't come. I looked for you, in the tents, in the bushes. I had no idea what might have happened." He clenched his jaw as he sucked in breath. "And then I saw Rosalie." He gave a low whistle. "She can be a looker when she cleans up."

"Ben!" She scowled at him as he grinned, ignoring her heated look.

"I asked for you. I begged her to tell me where you were, if you were okay. She in return tried to throw every girl on the island my way." He laughed a little, seeing Ariel's' expression. "Your sister is nothing if not tenacious. She tried to feed me drink, she sweet-talked girls for me, I had them lining up." He shook his head, his ears flashing red.

Ariel bit her tongue, not wanting to ask the question that was hovering above them.

"Sometime in the night she disappeared. She went off with a Watcher. I don't know why, but he looked familiar."

"Of course, he would. We saw them all on the stage that day."

Ben nodded, seemingly unconvinced.

"Why did she go with The Watcher?"

"I don't know, I didn't ask. He is a man, after all…"

"She wouldn't…"

Ben shrugged. "She found me last night, and she asked me how my week has been. I told her it was lonely without you. I begged her to tell me where you were. She wanted to know why I hadn't mated in five days. I told her she knew why. She asked me if I wanted to be taken."

"What did you say?"

His brow furrowed as his mouth turned grim. "I'd rather be taken by force as I'd never break my promise to you."

They fell silent for a moment, his words heavy and dark like a passing cloud. Ariel's pulse quickened as she wrenched her eyes from his and raked her fingers along his chest.

He closed his eyes and shook his head. "I asked for you again and she finally told me you were sick. I had to get to you, to see you were okay."

"I must have passed her test because she gave me something. A pill. It made me violently ill. My stomach felt like it was ripping apart from the inside, and when I lay on the ground writhing, Rosalie said it was a present from Mama Beth."

Ariel snorted at that.

"I do not know how, but your mother wields much power. She must have used much of it, for us." He pulled Ariel closer to him. "She loves you very much. Ariel, you were right. You did tell me so."

Ariel shook her head, trying to understand all he was saying.

"The Watchers came. Rosalie told them I was too sick and needed to be sent home. They wouldn't want all their guests sick. They gave me a medical pass. Rosalie promised to arrange my transport home. She must have bribed the oarsmen because they brought me here."

"Bribe? How?"

"You know how, Ariel."

Ariel fell silent.

"Was she okay?"

"You'll have to ask her when she gets back." He grazed her cheek with his knuckles. "The oarsmen will wait for me till midnight and then they will take me home. We have these fifteen hours. But I must stay hidden. You know the penalty."

"I do." She nodded.

"So, what should we do with our time? You know I can't leave this room at all. Maybe not even your bed." He gripped her tight and pulled her body close.

He tasted like the salt water he had not long ago left behind, and his body was coated with light granulated sand.

"You filled my bed with sand."

"There was an entire beach between me and your bed."

"So, it's my bed you were after all along?"

"Do you know how hard my bed is back on Dagon?"

"Can't say I'm surprised. You need a hard mattress to go with that thick head of yours."

"This thick head rolled around in the sand all night trying to get to you." He flipped her over and put his weight onto her, holding her down.

"You're an animal."

"And I made you a promise to share all my fleas." With that he put his hand to his hair and shook out a small pile of fine sand that coated Ariel's head, pillows and chest. She wriggled beneath him, shrieking. "What? Is this not part of the deal?" he jested as she tried to buck beneath him.

"No, you beast, get off me," she shrieked as he held her. His forehead leaning onto hers, his eyes locked with hers, his smile alight.

He brushed her lips with his, her body falling still. His

delicate, exquisite kiss deep and hungry, she pulled away from him and fell into a coughing fit, her small body contorting as her throat corded with the effort.

"Sorry." His face had grown darker.

"I'm fine, just a little tired, just a little hungry and now, my mouth is full of sand." She licked her teeth and grimaced. "I need to go wash it out."

"Is that an invitation? I would love to wash the sand from you."

Ariel's heart skipped a beat as she felt the heat rise to her face. She pushed away from him. Sitting up slowly, she stood up on shaky legs. Coughing once more, her body crumpled in two.

Ben caught her arm, a look of concern on his face.

"I'm okay." She gave him a weak smile as a fine rain of sand sprinkled onto her floor. "Not sure you signed up to share any of my germs, though."

"I signed up for everything. Now sit down and wait here."

"Ben! Ben, you can't leave this room. You can't be seen." She called to him with a harsh whisper, her voice straining as he poked his head beyond the door.

"Coast is clear. I'll be right back. Don't move!"

"Ben! Ben," she called to the empty doorway as another coughing fit took hold.

She heard the taps groaning and the splash of heavy water.

When he returned, Ben held his arm out to her. He led her to the bathroom. The room veiled in steam, which rose like mist form the porcelain tub. Small droplets attached themselves to the tiles and walls in a thin layer of perspiration.

Ben pushed Ariel against the wall and reached for her blouse, he tugged on the material.

"No." She pushed his hand away.

"Let me help you." His chocolate eyes radiated fierce, uncompromising concern.

Ariel screwed her eyes shut and sighed. When she reopened them, she was met with his unnerving gaze, and reluctantly lifted her hands above her head.

Ben peeled the tight material which clung to her body like ivy. Her breasts bounced about in their new-found freedom. He risked a peek before tugging at her underwear. Her chest rose and fell as she breathed heavily. Exposed. Vulnerable. Aroused. Ben released her of the thin cloth.

She clutched at his hand as he guided her to the bath and steadied her as she climbed in, releasing her so she could sink into the water. He sat on the edge of the bath, trying to memorise each one of her curves and mounds, her scars and dimples, and imperfections as she disappeared beneath the film of translucent water. He watched as her flesh tinted pink with heat.

Ariel surfaced, her flushed skin plump. Ben squeezed a bead of shampoo onto his palm and begun to rake the lotion through her wet hair, the strands falling, slippery and soapy through his hands. She craned her neck to him, her face beginning to slack and lose shape as she allowed him this small pleasure.

He inhaled the fruity fragrance as he scrubbed and massaged until a thick layer of foam had formed. Filling the hand bucket, he rinsed her hair, allowing the water to cascade around her until it ran clear.

Ben grabbed the washcloth and reached for Ariel's arm. Ever so slowly, washing the length of her, her lips parted as he kneaded her body, savouring the silky feel of her skin under his calloused fingers.

When he was done, he pulled her out of the water and watched as it cascaded down in rivulets. He wrapped a towel around her and led her back to her room.

Ben watched her dress. Long limbs slipping into lose fabric. Her long black hair leaving a wet snaky trail on the white singlet. "Thank you," she whispered.

He nodded silently, lost in thought.

"I feel better."

"You smell better." He crinkled his nose, his eyes alight with humour.

"At least one of us does."

He raised an arm and sniffed his armpit. He grimaced and flinched. "You're not wrong."

They laughed as Ariel inched toward the door.

"Where are you going? I thought we were going to spend the day together."

"Getting away from you and your obnoxious body odour."

"Hey," he pouted, "that's not fair."

She turned back to him and blew him a kiss. "I'll be right back. I just have to go get something."

"I don't want you to get anything. I just want you to rest."

"And I will as soon as I get back."

"From where?"

"Just stay in my room. Don't be seen. I'll be back soon." She blew him another kiss and gave no other explanations.

He lay on her bed, listening to the quite descend on the house. He felt at home in a way he hadn't in years. Like this place had known him as much as he had known it, like it had missed his presence.

He inhaled Ariel's scent that had been soaked into the pillow. Sweet flower and musty morning breath. His groin ached from being denied once more. Images of her bare flesh in his palm reignited his yearning for her. Standing up uncomfortably, he paced the room, avoiding the window.

He heard the voices as they filtered through the open

window, chattering and loud. Almost familiar. He dove under the bed, gluing his back to the wall. Remaining motionless.

The door creaked as it was pushed open "Ben?" He heard Ariel's whisper and watched her bare feet covered in sand as she stepped toward the bed.

"Down here," he whispered and waited as she squatted down to find him.

"What are you doing?"

"I heard voices... I didn't think the sheet would provide enough cover." He winked at her and she shook her head. "Are you referring to your…" She nudged towards his groin which she noticed was still swollen.

He shrugged in return and winked at her. "I can't help what you do to me."

"I need you to get rid of that and wait here."

He pulled himself from under the bed and gave her a toothy grin. "No food references?"

"Just put it away!"

She watched as he closed his eyes, breathing deeply. His face grimaced and the bulge in his pants begun to dissolve.

"Okay, now what?" He seemed to be straining.

"Just sit on the bed. I'll be back in a sec." With that, she bolted from the room, leaving him once more to wonder.

He didn't make it to the bed as he heard hushed voices and the weight of feet on the tired wood floor.

He looked to the threshold where just beyond, he was met with a face he had dreamed about for years.

"Mom?" he called, running to the woman who stood open-mouthed at the doorway.

"Ben?" She stood perplexed as the large man rushed towards her. He stopped right in front of her. The older woman looked into his face, brushing his chin with her hardened fingers, tugging slightly on his hair, studying the brown eyes.

"Ben," she cried, her tears slicing her otherwise beautiful features as she threw herself onto him. He wrapped her in his arms, his own tears stinging his eyes.

"How?" His mother looked at him, bewildered.

"I'll let you two catch up." Ariel beamed at the pair and made her way to the kitchen.

Ariel's stomach growled as hunger gnawed at her. She scrambled some eggs and burned toast. Made juice and coffee, all the while hearing drifts of conversation from her room. Light giggles and sad laughter.

She piled everything onto a tray and carried it to her room.

She watched them, side by side, her hands laced in his, creases of laughter on both their faces. They were glowing.

She placed the tray on the floor, breaking the spell.

Mama Cath held Ben in a long embrace then placed a soft kiss on his cheek, whispering something in his ear. His mouth split into a smile and he held her one last time.

As she shuffled to the door, she took Ariel in her arms. "Thank you, Ariel, for this gift. I'll show myself out." She took one lingering look at her boy, who was now a man, and left behind her an empty silence broken by the gentle clap of the front door as it shut.

"Oh, Ariel," Ben choked on his words as he held her. His lips finding hers in desperation, he clung to her, tears running down his face.

When they broke free, his eyes glistened with tears and were creased with joy. "Ariel, I... Thank you."

He slunk to the bed, his emotions in turmoil. She lay by his side, soothing him until her stomach reminded her of her plight. He chuckled at the sound.

"Better get some food into you if we're going to make you better."

Nightfall rolled over the horizon and brought with it a cool breeze that swept across the silent house. The hours had slipped through their hands like water, as they tried to hold on to each moment. She found herself often in his embrace and his heavy lips on hers, demanding, wanting, extracting from her desire.

Wrapped in his arms, his warmth against hers, Ariel pulled away from his mouth, wiping away the moisture and grinning. "So, I know how you can repay me."

"Repay you?"

"Yes."

"What for?"

"For this morning."

"I thought that was a gift." He raised an eyebrow. "And anyway, I gave you a bath, didn't I?"

"Exactly."

"Ariel," he sighed, "I'm going to need some help understanding."

"You saw mine… now…"

"Show you? My beast? Or was it a noodle? Or a sausage?" He laughed as she burned a shade of pink.

"Yes," she bit her lip, "I want to see it."

"*It?*"

"Yes." She pushed his shoulder, biting her lip.

"If I recall correctly, you have already had the pleasure. Twice."

"Those times didn't count."

"How so?"

"The first time you were thirteen, and the other time it was dark."

"But you did sneak a few peeks." He winked at her as pink gave way to dark red.

"Oh, forget about it." She rolled off him. He grabbed her and rolled on top of her, pinning her down.

"So fiery, Ariel. So impatient," he whispered in a husky voice as he pulled her lips apart with his. "I've been waiting for years for you to ask."

He battled his way through the sheet and swaggered to the centre of her room where he stood to his full height, hands on his hips, his commanding visage betrayed only by his clenched jaw.

They stared at one another in silence, each challenging the other.

Ariel crawled from the bed and approached him.

"So, this is how you want to play it?"

"I'm only playing by your rules." He tried to sound cocky but the tremble in his voice gave away far more than he had intended.

Ariel circled around him as he stood frozen, only his chest heaving. Rising and falling.

His face twitched as she landed a hand on his chest. A finger wrapping against a single black hair, tugging at it slightly, goosebumps erupting on his skin. Ariel continue to circle, her hand dragging along the length of his abdomen, as she felt his every muscle tighten beneath her touch. She caressed his upper arm, tracing it from his shoulder to his elbow and back again.

With the tips of her fingers, she felt the strength of his back, tracing each dip and scar. His breath became more laboured under her touch. She allowed herself time to wonder and explore his body, stroking his soft skin as she once again faced him, her fingers lingering on his heart, the beat reaching out to her.

Slipping her hands to his shorts, he gasped, and then as if paralysed, held his breath. Pushing down ever so slightly, his body stiffened further, as if he was made of marble. She lifted the fabric over the mounting bulge beneath and set him free, allowing his shorts to fall to his feet.

They stood for a single moment, motionless, before Ben reached for her, making short work of her clothing.

He fell onto her and she moved readily to his touch. His hands stroked and circled.

"I want to be your mate. Now," she whispered to Ben and he stilled, his hand floating just above her. He pulled away from her despite his body screaming for hers.

"No. We can't."

"Why? I'm saying yes, I'm ready."

"No." He shook his head and shied away from her, lifting his body from hers.

Wild-eyed, flushed, she scowled at him pulling the sheet across her naked body.

"Don't be angry at me, Ariel. I am only doing what we agreed."

"But I am giving myself to you. Don't you want me?" Her voice was clipped.

"More than anything else in this world." He ran a hand through his hair. His teeth gleamed as he clenched his jaw in desperation. "But if we do this, I may never get a chance to see you again. You know the risk we take. I can't stand not seeing you again." He reached for her, but she flinched from his touch.

"Wouldn't you rather have a child? With me? What if we try on our fifth encounter and naught comes of it? What if we will lose our only chance?"

"Have you not been listening to anything I have said to you? I do not want to give you a child if *I* cannot be a part of its life."

"So, you would rather have me not having any part of you?"

"Ariel?"

"Is this how it's meant to be? You, on your island and I on mine? Alone? No pieces of you, while you go back to Ishmin, cycle after cycle, year after year, and try again with another?

Others? How could I live, knowing you have given yourself to someone else? That another might carry your seed, your child?"

"Ariel…"

"If you will not do this with me today, you will not do this with me at all! I will seek another. I'd rather have a child to love, to cling onto than nothing at all. The consequences for me outweigh yours tenfold."

"Ariel, don't say that."

"I mean it!"

"Ariel." He spoke through clenched teeth.

"Come here and do what needs to be done. I know you want to. I have seen how you struggle each time you touch me. Touch me now. Please." Her voice quivered.

"Ariel." He softened.

"Please?" Tears welled in her eyes.

"I can't." He looked away from her small body which seemed to be shrinking before him.

"You won't!" She tugged at the sheet, her face reddening, embarrassment and anger taking over.

"Not like this, Ariel. I…"

"You need to leave." Her eyes were blazing.

"Ariel…"

"Go! Go now!" she screeched.

"Ariel, please, just listen…"

"Get out!" she screamed.

Bursting from the bed, he grabbed his shorts and pivoted on his heel, taking off without a backwards glance.

Ariel lay on the bed, red hot tears soaking into her pillow.

A riel was sour when her mother returned.

"Ariel?" Mama Beth stepped into her darkened room. "What are you still doing in bed?"

She didn't answer.

"Why did you not go and greet your sister this morning? She was tired and needed help."

"You went, didn't you?" The heated reply came from beneath the sheet.

"She'll stay with her boys for one more night before returning home. She was exhausted."

Ariel remained silent.

"What's going on, Ariel? Did you not like the gift I sent you? I thought you would be happier to see me."

"Leave me alone."

Mama Beth sighed and sat on the bed, the mattress dipping with her added weight. She tugged at the sheet until Ariel relented, poking her head out and facing her mother. "What happened?"

"Nothing." She sucked in breath. Her cheeks burned with salt tears.

"Did he hurt you?"

Ariel said nothing.

"Don't say I didn't tell you so." Mama Beth stood up.

"It's not what you think."

"It never is. Now get your sorry ass up and get ready for the day. Just because your feelings are hurt doesn't mean chores don't need to be done." With that, she left Ariel's room.

PROMISES

Three months is a long time to carry angst and anger about, but Ariel had no problem carrying the coal which ignited to a red ember each time she thought of Ben's rejection.

She skulked around, being short with her mom and her sister. Mia, whose belly was swollen and stretched, tried to placate her friend thinking it was not getting pregnant that was depressing her.

When not at work, Ariel climbed the cliff face and watched the beach until the sun disappeared. She would then sneak back home, avoiding her mother, and would beg for sleep.

Each time she pulled the sheet over her head, she remembered the look on his face. His arms on her skin turning cold, the spark dying out.

The constant knot in her belly was making her insane. Only one more night to go.

She threw her small bag on the cot and inhaled deeply. Brushing a hand through her hair, she straightened her dress and tapped her cheeks, hoping to infuse some colour into them. Her mother, as usual, had done a beautiful and delicate job with her make up. She was ready.

She willed her legs to carry her to the meeting area, coming to a stop at the elevated entrance, and surveyed the crowd on the dance floor, clenching and unclenching her hands.

She spotted Ben, who locked eyes with her. He smiled and waved pulling away from the bar. Ariel ignored him, searching.

She found Liam sandwiched between two brunettes. They could have been sisters. Ariel grimaced at the thought. Sashaying onto the dance floor, she thrust herself through the undulating dancers. Ariel licked her lips, the red shimmering in the flickering light.

Catching Liam's eye, she gave him a shy smile. Like lightning, he pushed away from the sisters and bolted his way to her, his hips oscillating in jerky movements.

"Hello again." He was cautious in his approach.

"Hi." Her voice as musky and low. She saw the light change in Liam's eyes.

He took a step closer, his hips now falling into rhythm with hers.

"Ariel." Ben's hand landed hard on her shoulder and he spun her around.

"Don't touch me," she hissed at him as Liam's hand travelled along her waist, encouraged by her cool demeanour to his rival.

"Ariel."

"Go away, Ben."

"You heard the lady. Go away, pretty boy," Liam chirped in as he glued his body to Ariel, his groin to her buttock.

"You wouldn't want The Watchers to think you're doing something against her will now."

"Ariel?" Ben tried again as Liam drew Ariel against him, his hand roaming the side of her body, resting just below her bosom.

Ariel remained silent as Liam kissed her neck. Ben noticed the slight grimace and the way her body tensed at the foreign touch.

"Is this what you really want?"

"You know what I want, now go away," she shot, her voice pinched. A sudden pit opened at her belly as she saw him flinch at her words.

Without further protest Ben turned around and left them. Ariel felt Liam's mouth stretched in a wide grin.

"Let's get out of here," Liam whispered in her ear, his enthusiasm growing. She could feel his growth through her dress and tried to keep from grimacing. Her stomach churned as he pulled her way from the dance floor and towards one of the secluded bungalows along the beach.

"I'll be honest. I thought I was never going to have you. I can't wait to get you out of that dress." He almost broke into a run.

Ariel found herself looking over her shoulder. This was what she wanted, what she had waited for the last three months, or perhaps her entire life. To erase every trace of Ben from her life. This would break him. This would make him stay away.

This wasn't what she wanted.

Liam pulled her by the hand, his grip tightening, nails digging into her skin, almost dragging her.

"Slow down. We have all night." She pulled against his grip, breathless in their half-trot.

"Yes, we do." He halted and jerked on her hand, forcing her body against his. "But I have been waiting almost a year for you, and I don't want to wait a minute longer. See what you do to me?" Crudely he pulled at the elastic of his pants, baring himself to her. His erection hard against his skin.

Ariel looked away, her heart thrashing in terror.

They arrived at the small bungalow. Liam yanked her smaller form through the open arched frame. There were no doors and two large windows.

The Watchers must watch.

A bed rested in the centre of the room, and a single chair was pushed against the wall.

Not allowing either of the time to catch their breaths, Liam reached for the clasp behind her neck and tugged it forcefully. The fabric came loose around her shoulders, and she grabbed at it, collecting it and holding it firmly across her chest.

"Oh, come now, no need to be shy with me, Ariel. I want to see you. Let go of the dress."

She stood frozen, clutching the thin fabric.

"Okay, let me go first." He reached for his pants and removed them, throwing them carelessly across the room. She looked at his arousal, jutting from within the tangle of pubic hair.

"Do you like what you see?" He took a step closer as Ariel backed away. "Now it's your turn, beautiful Ariel. Let me see you. I have been dreaming of you since the day I first saw you."

She let her dress drop, her hands screening her chest.

Liam studied her body. "Hands down now."

Ariel's chest seemed to cave as she allowed her hands to fall to her side, her bare chest drawing a gasp of excitement from Liam.

"Even better than I imagined." He licked his lips drawing closer.

Tracing a finger along her chin, he followed the contours of her neck, down between her breasts, coming to a halt at her lacy underpants. "Exquisite," he whispered as his eyes sparkled.

Ariel stood motionless as he peeled her last barrier from her body, her skin breaking into goosebumps as her stomach protested, twisting in cruel knots.

Liam seized her by the wrist and led her over to the chair. In a daze, she noticed his gentle push on her back coaxing her, so that she bent over. Reaching over her, he placed her hands on either side of the chair, so that they were fully stretched out. She was completely exposed.

"Oh, you're a sight. I'm going to take such good care of you." His hand wandered to her hips and her stomach heaved.

Ariel shot up and sucked in a deep breath. "Liam, I don't want to do this." A single tear ran down her cheek and her hands clasped at her nakedness, hiding it once more.

"What are you talking about?" His playful manner fell away like her discarded dress.

"I've changed my mind. I don't want you."

"I don't think you know what you want. Just let me show you how good I can make you feel." He stepped towards her again.

"Please, Liam." Her voice trembled as her wild eyes let loose tears.

"I promise to make it quick." He closed the distance between them. "No need to cry."

"She said no." Ben's voice at the door sounded almost relieved.

"You? Again? Did she not tell you to go away?" Liam swung around, his face rigid.

"Pretty sure that's what she is telling you to do now, *Liam*."

"I'm pretty sure that's none of your business, pretty boy."

"I will make it my business, and The Watchers' business if you do not leave right now."

Liam's jaw clamped tight. His face twisted into a scowl as he pushed past Ariel, fishing for his shorts. He grabbed them and ploughed into Ben as he marched out.

Ben looked at Ariel, his mouth a severe line, his eyes plagued with tortured emotion, hers swollen with tears. Without a word, he turned around and left.

"Ben." She called after him, but he had already been swallowed up by the darkness.

Ariel found her clothes through a cascade of tears and dressed quickly. She ran onto the sand looking for Ben.

She found him sitting on a rock, his face lit by the full moon, tinting his features in silver and blue. His shoulders slouched over his bowed frame as he clinched onto his legs, remaining motionless.

"Ben."

"Go away, Ariel." He didn't turn to her.

"I'm sorry." Her voice quivered. "I was angry... I was stupid..."

"With him? Out of all people?" He gave her a look raked with disdain.

"Ben... I'm sorry."

"I thought you understood. I thought we had a deal. You can't go and change the rules whenever it suits you."

"I..."

"I don't want to hear about it, Ariel. Not now."

"Ben..."

"I need to think, and you need to leave." His body slumped as if deflated.

She put a hand on his arm and he jerked it away. "Just go." He turned away from her, once more watching the crashing waves.

Ariel studied his face. Pain and anger were etched into the hardened surface. "I'm sorry," she whispered as she slid from the rock, ignoring the tightening knot in her stomach.

Forcing her heavy legs to move, she lumbered back to her tent.

⟁

A riel had scoured Ishmin for three days and still found no trace of Ben. She had visited his tent and was met with laughter and taunting when she asked for him. She was told he had not slept there and was probably out enjoying himself. The insinuation, accompanied by suggestive gestures, brought bile to her throat. She had searched along the beaches and in every bungalow, interrupting copulating couples in her search. She climbed to the caves and looked from the hilltop. Still, she could not find him.

Defeated, she let the days slip by. With two days before she would be plucked from the safety of her tent and Taken before the crowd, she could feel The Watchers' eyes on her. Their stares weighed on her like lead chains.

Her coffee tasted bitter, the breakfast stale as she nibbled at the morsels on the end of her fork, forcing herself to eat. The growing pit in her belly had grown, leaving no space for anything but sorrow. Her anxiety grew. She was broken. She had hurt Ben with her words, with her actions, and he would give her no chances to explain, to beg his forgiveness, to repent. He was all but gone.

She avoided Liam's cruel scowls and openly aggressive gestures at her and withdrew, staying in her tent, going out only to eat, drink and cleanse. She winced each time she wondered if Ben would hurt her in the same way that she had hurt him, the pit in her stomach expanding, threatening to swallow up what was left of her world. The thought of no longer having a claim to him brought only fresh tears.

When she woke up on the morning of the sixth day, she found Ben lying on the floor next to her cot. She didn't dare move, didn't want to wake the still body. Instead she took him in, the slight rise and fall of his chest, the slightly parted lips and the mop of hair that fell just over his eyes.

Her heart jolted when he stirred.

"Hi." She gave him a tentative smile when he opened his eye.

"Hi." His expression was blank.

Ariel swallowed the lump in her throat and waited for him to speak. Ben pushed himself off the sand, his back a white blanket of fine sediment.

"Why Liam? Out of all the men here?" He grimaced. His face drawn, and light blue circles outlined his puffy eyes.

"Because he would have hurt you the most." Her face fell into her hand and she shook her head.

"He would have hurt you, too." Ben let the words hang in the air.

"Ben, I _"

"I know."

"It's just not fair, the thought of not having you. It cuts like a knife. It hurts to breathe. I'm not cut out to be without you."

"Ariel."

"I'm sorry, I've been so selfish."

He didn't dispute her proclamation.

"I know we made promises. And I know you were only keeping yours, but I got so scared, I would be left with nothing. I don't know how to navigate this world without you in it. I don't know how to have your child without you by my side. I don't know if it's best to just be alone, never tasting your flesh, never truly being with you, then to have you for just one week and never again."

She pushed off the bed. "The way you made me feel that night, the way you looked at me, I knew you wanted the same thing, and after you denied me, I was humiliated, ashamed." She sucked in a shaky breath.

"Maybe you didn't want me as much as I wanted you, maybe I was all wrong all along."

At that, Ben straightened up and buried his head on her lap, clutching her thighs. "No, Ariel. All I want is you. I have waited a lifetime for you, and I didn't want to lose you. Besides, if you would have fallen pregnant when you were not on the island, we both would have been doomed..."

He clutched her body as he buried his face in her neck.

"I'm sorry, Ben."

"I know." He kissed her tears. "I know, we have wasted so much precious time. Now let's put on our show. They're watching."

"I thought you were angry with me."

"I am. But I still love you, and I can never let another have you."

Ben pulled her to him, onto him. His mouth on hers, desperate, drawing from her pleasure, demanding satiation. His heart reverberated against her as his hands travelled the length of her, his fingers rippling her skin, exploring her flesh.

She unclasped her dress and allowed the fabric to fall around her shoulders, unheeded, like a faded flower. Needing her bare skin against him, he tugged harshly, leaving her exposed, just the lace underwear showing glimpses of what lie beneath.

He slowed down, savouring her, tasting her, studying every inch of her body with his long, nimble fingers, extracting from her low moans and gasps as he explored her figure.

He kissed her, swallowing her joy, her delight, her love and she devoured his lips with need and satisfaction. His heat pooled between them as he clutched at her skin, grunting and moving against her.

When they had settled, he clipped the dress back on. He

watched the light fabric as it fell along her delicate body, soaking their sins, hiding their secret.

"Ben, that was – "Ariel did not know how to continue. Her mind reeling with pleasure, chagrined confusion as she sat up and pulled her knees into her.

"It was beautiful. Ariel, you are beautiful." He kissed her, willing her to see.

She nodded, thanking him silently.

"Will it be like that when we... when you...?"

"I hope so." He kissed her lightly.

They stepped out of her tent, the bright sun burning in their hazy eyes. Hand in hand, they strolled along the beach, their steps lighter as the weight they had both carried lifted.

Sitting on the sand, Ariel started, "What are we going to do?"

"I still don't know."

She nodded into the silence that surrounded them.

19

THE WATCHERS

The Keep Seeker scanned the open book before her and examined Ariel. She stood up and rounded the table, her hunched form clutching onto Ariel's hand. She tugged on the dress and pinned the red star to the fabric then patted her arm.

Sitting back down, she scanned the book once more. "Maybe it's time to seek another mate, the *one* you have recorded seems to be problematic." Ariel cringed as her stomach tumbled. She nodded meekly at the greying woman and shuffled away. Glares and looks followed her everywhere, both pity and predatory.

Women took two steps away from her as if her barrenness was somehow contagious. Whispers followed her like a cold breeze. The star had an opposite effect on the men. As if it was a scent, primal and old, which invited every male into her circle sniffing for their opportunity to strike.

Ariel brushed by them to her tent, knowing all too well that tonight would be the night. In Ben's arms, they would fulfill all the promises they had made and their love finally shared.

As she navigated her way to the meeting area, bright light

and loud music glided through the air around her. She stood scanning the crowd, her hands restlessly pulling at her dress. She waited. Ben wasn't there. She weaved her way to the bar, scanning the dance floor. His familiar shape was not there. Her heart raced as she returned to their meeting place, pacing, waiting.

When he had failed to show up, she faltered, her heart sank as a chill ran through her. She strode away toward the beach, her breath heavy, a rock lodged in her throat. She could feel the sniffing of the others, like a pack of wolves.

The sand felt course beneath her feet as she ran, sand spewing around her as she lifted her feet, bolting. And then she saw him.

A silver statue in the moonlight. Her entire being shivered, her heart threatening to burst from her chest.

She halted.

"Ben?"

He turned to her, his face covered in darkness. He made no move towards her.

Taking a few tentative steps, she reached out to him. "Ben?"

"Ariel." He whispered to her. "Don't come any closer."

"Ben."

Ignoring his request, she slammed into his body, and he wrapped her in his strong arms. "Why didn't you come? I thought…" She looked to his face and her mouth fell open. "Ben?" She pushed away from his frame so that she could examine him, her eyes bulging. "What happened?"

"Just a scratch." His eyes grew dark as she brushed his mangled face with the tips of her fingers. He winced at the touch.

"Ben, what happened?" Her voice was strained as she took him in. A broad rough scar had been carved into his face, meandering from his left eye to his jaw. Whatever had caused it was blunt and it was clear that the injury wasn't treated. His body was littered with bruises of various shades of purple, black and yellow. "Who did this?"

"Everything we do has a consequence."

"Liam?"

He nodded silently.

"I did this?" Her voice fell as she screwed up her face.

Ben took a step toward her, slipping a hand around her. "No." His other hand floated to her back, coming to rest between her shoulder blades where her skin was bare and soft.

"Are you okay?" Her throat dry.

"I am now, that you are here."

"Let's get you to your tent. You need to rest. You need to heal."

"No."

"Ben."

"No. All I need is you, tonight, now." His eyes implored as he found her lips. They stood kissing among the beach and the moon and the waves. A sweet delicate kiss that carried with it promise and hid within anticipation. Ariel's hand slipped into Ben's as he pulled her to a waiting bungalow, a slight limp to his stride as he held his damaged chest.

"Ben," she breathed his name, "are you sure? You're hurt."

"Yes." His avid eyes burned as his gaze dipped to her lips. "I am not waiting another day, another minute, another second. I want you, Ariel, now."

Ben stood over her, his looming body stoic in the moon-light, as they breached the doorway.

"No more show. It's time I make good on my promises." His hungry eyes intense as he stalked forward, Ariel retreating on shaky legs.

She found the edge of the bed and sank down to it, trapped between the softness of the sheets and his hard body. Ben stared at her, his jaw locked, his fists pumping at his sides.

She found the centre of the bed. Her breaths uneven, pulsed around the room as he prowled up her body.

Her hands fell about him, exploring his thick shoulders and strong arms, clutching to his brawny back. Pulling his body against hers. Her light touch caressing every bump and scar, weaving among the light sprinkling of hair in his chest and jaw.

Ben tugged at her dress and the fabric fell away, delicately, as if he was peeling a juicy orange, her flesh beneath flushed and needy. He glimpsed the beads of sweat along her chest, the triangle of dark hair between her legs.

When his fingers tugged at the elastic of the lacy undergarment, she did not stop him. Ever so slowly, he shed the last of her barriers and revealed her womanhood. She was glorious and beautiful even as she tried to cover herself up.

"Don't." He kissed away her worry, drinking in her nudity. "You are beautiful, Ariel."

His hands trembled, sweaty, as he removed his shorts, and she allowed him to nestle himself between her. His skin burned, his movements suddenly clumsy, slow, uncertain.

Ben gave her a stiff but reassuring smile. "Are you ready?" A tender whisper, a scorching look.

She nodded stiffly, her face the colour of freshly plucked strawberries.

The music from the party seemed to dim, her eyes veiled, her cheeks flushed, her heart beating as she wrapped herself around him, and tangled limbs and hair and sweat, they met together at last.

She allowed him to lay waste to her body as she savoured his ministrations on her bare flesh. Fingers and tongue as the rhythm of her heart surpassed that of her thighs until she let go. Her body alight under his touch.

They lay panting. Heaving chests and glistening, bodies still entangled. He rolled from her and she placed her head on his chest, avoiding his eyes. She watched his manhood inch back into the safety of his pubic hair, no longer needed for the task.

"Are you okay?" His gentle voice hoarse, she could hear the uncertainty.

Ariel looked up to him and met his eyes. "I am." She leaned in, brushing his lips with hers, reassuring.

"Did I hurt you?" Still dismayed.

Her hands curled around his midriff. "A little," she whispered.

"I'll try to be more gentle next time."

"Next time?" She eyed him demurely. "What makes you think that I will let that *thing* come near me again?" A hint of a smile crossed her face.

Even as she looked, the small nub came out from behind its hairy hiding place. It twitched and jolted to life, once more engorged. Ariel giggled, enjoying the thrill of having so much control over Ben's body by merely looking at him.

"I don't think you're going to have any choice in the matter." He grinned boyishly and she shoved an elbow into him.

He winced, his injured body remembering its pain.

"Sorry." She grimaced and kissed his bruised limb. "Is that better?"

He nodded then flinched once more.

Ariel kissed him again. "And that?"

He nodded, "It hurts here too." He pointed to his chin a black mark decorated his jaw.

Ariel lay her lips on his broken skin, her eyes welling with tears.

"I'm sorry..." She begun as he swallowed her words with his mouth.

She met him once more in his need.

"**E**nough! I've got nothing left to give."

"Quitter!" she jibed at him as they lay bare, one tousled in the other.

"You have become quite the fiend." He kissed her sweaty forehead and sucked in breath as she wriggled above him.

"We've wasted so much time. And soon we will be out of time." Her voice faltered. "You must give this gift to me, so that *if* we cannot be together, I will always have a piece of you." She clamped her thighs against his waist.

At her words, he fell silent and she felt his body twitch. His muscles suddenly rigid.

"Don't say that. There cannot be another way for us. I cannot live without you."

"Nor I without you." She kissed his chest, which seemed to be holding breath. "But…"

"No, no buts." He pushed her off and lay her on to her back, her bare body glistening with moisture. "Imagine if it's already happening. If deep inside of you a part of me is already growing."

He trailed a long finger to her navel and circled her belly button. He lowered his head to her abdomen. "Grow," he whispered as if wanting her belly to swell before his eyes.

She giggled and pushed him off, her cheeks flushed red. "Let's go swim."

"You go, I'm exhausted. Honestly, I don't know how you have the energy to still move around."

"See? This is why we are the superior sex." She stuck out her tongue at him and his gaze swept along her naked body. He took in the tanned complexion long ago kissed by the sun in places. Contrasted with untouched white along her swollen breasts, the nipples firm, surrounded by a cushion of soft flesh. Her curved shape edged by slightly protruding hip bones. Her long slim legs that converged over a small area, tucked away between her strong thighs, but that already held so much power over him.

He tried to etch every inch of her into his memory as she slipped into her clothes. "Come with me."

"I can't." He winked at her. "But don't take too long. I'm sure I will recover quickly."

"You better." She giggled as she ran from the bungalow towards the rolling sea.

He watched as her shape disappeared beyond the big blue and his eyes welled with tears. His silent sobs swallowed like ships on the stormy seas.

I n six nights and days she had gotten to know his body in a way she never thought she would.

Though her shyness had not altogether dissipated, she was aware of his constant fascination with her female form, and his eager response to it. The bloom of youth and the need so long forsaken to them, stretched before them, alluring and intriguing like the open sea.

When she woke, she found him hunched over the edge of the bed, his face drawn as it rested in his palm.

"Are you ok?"

"I'm scared." He turned to face her, his brows hovering low over his brooding eyes.

"Of what?"

"Of losing you." He shot from the bed and walked to the arched entrance of the bungalow.

"That's never going to happen."

He didn't answer. She rose from the bed, clutching the sheet to her body.

"Ben. It will be okay."

Reaching for her, he murmured her name into her neck. "Ariel." His desperation leaked from the touch of his skin as he searched for comfort within her. Her taste, her touch, her smell a balm to his ache.

As evening set, they watched the blue horizon turn a deep crimson. They sat hushed, wishing time to slow down.

"Once we do this, there is no backing out." Her voice cracked as she spoke.

"I know."

"Are you sure you want to do this?"

"Ariel, I have been sure since the first day I met you." He pulled her closer, his body hard against her softness.

"I love you, Ben."

"I love you, too, Ariel."

They shared a chaste kiss, in fear of spilling out into the world.

20

CALL TO COUNCIL

"Who are The Watchers, Mama Beth?" asked an eight-year-old Ariel.

"Where did you hear about them?"

"In the nursery, Mama Rachel talked about them."

Mama Beth took a long drag from her cigarette and sat down on the porch, patting the wood beside her where Ariel perched her small body. She inhaled her mother's sweet smoke and leaned into the woman.

"The Watchers are the keepers of our society, they are the keepers of our secrets, our histories and our rules."

"And who put them in charge?"

"We did."

"How?"

"The islands have their leaders. They are not formal nor are they named but they are known."

"Like you?"

"Don't interrupt," she said harshly, not denying the question. "When they come of age, they may choose to leave their island and go to Ishmin or islands like it in the four territories. There, they will grow old while keeping traditions and rules alive."

"But how do they do that if they are so far?"

"You don't let up, do you, kid?"

Ariel shook her head vigorously as she inhaled another whiff of the cherry tobacco.

"The leaders of each island are their eyes and ears. They can choose to deal with matters alone or to bring forth messages to The Watchers who consult among themselves, consult the ancient histories, the new future and decide the fate of all involved."

Ariel considered her words. "But what if you do not like the judgment?"

"You can stand and be tried."

"How do you do that?"

Her mother sighed. "You call an assembly of Watchers and you ask for someone to stand for you."

Ariel saw the signs. Her mother's patience was wearing thin. "How do they do that?"

Her mother stood up, singling the conversation was over. She took the first step off the porch when Ariel grabbed her by the hand.

"One last question?" She looked at her desperately.

"Make it a quick one." Her mother sucked on her white roll-up, the tip burning in a bright orange ember.

"At what age do The Watchers leave?"

"At 65."

Ariel threw her arms around her mother and smiled. "That means we still have lots of time, then."

The eight-year-old beamed at the woman who softened and patted the child on the back.

"Plenty." She broke away and meandered down the path, leaving behind a trail of white smoke.

A riel's palms were clammy as she squeezed Ben's hand. The late evening sun bore down on them as they stood in the middle of the stage, the barren, wooden structure seeming worn and scuffed in the evening light, the magic of fire light and music having long since evaporated.

Ben stood still and solid as she quivered beside him. "We would like to summon the high council," Ariel called out into the air, knowing full well they were being watched.

An old man in a loin cloth appeared like smoke from behind a tree. A fringe of grey hair framed his wrinkled face. He took an ungainly step forward and his deep velvety voice washed over them. "Who calls this council?"

"Ariel, Daughter of Elizabeth and Benjen, son of Catherine."

"And what matter do you wish to bring before the council?"

Ariel stiffened, her legs threatening to give way. Finding strength in Ben's resolve, she called out, "We seek permission to marry."

It was as if every occupant on the island gasped, the wind seemed to die off and the world stilled for a second.

The Watcher nodded, his face grim. Ariel noticed the brown spots along his rough skin which hung from his bones like loose cloth. He brought two bony fingers to his mouth and whistled, the sound sharp and harsh.

From beyond the tree line, the whistle was taken up by another, fading in ferocity as it travelled from Watcher to Watcher, until it was heard no more.

A bell tolled across the island. The metallic and slow ring reverberated over the water. Ariel had never heard the sound before. She wondered if anyone in her lifetime had, as her heart jolted.

The sound brought with it the crowd. Murmurs of wonder carried, as men and women, some still in states of undress, streamed into the meeting area where Ben and Ariel stood, their hands laced, knuckles white, breaths held.

From above, appearing from the tree line and behind the rocks as if they were part of the island itself, begun to appear The Watchers. They encircled the arena from above and formed a human wall of dour faces.

The human wall opened up to allow a man and a woman to step through, the wall closing behind them.

Adorned in her red dress, The Watcher began, "I am The Watcher Tay, daughter of Audrey. Beside me stands the Watcher Eric, son of Clara." Her honeyed voice carried a note of venom as the crowd fell silent.

"Step forward Ariel, daughter of Elizabeth and Benjen, Son of Catherine"

The crowd that had closed around them rippled apart, allowing them to pass, as if rubbing shoulders with either might infect them with a lethal virus. Hand in hand, they stepped to the fore and faced The Watchers.

"What is it that you seek?" Tay's voice spilled over them, her lips taut.

Pushing her shoulders back and holding her head high, Ariel began. "We seek to be mates for life, promised only to one another."

Tay burst into laughter as the crowd gasped at her words. With the dwindling of her laughter, Tay lifted her hands, awaiting silence.

"If you choose to deprive yourself of the joy of mating with as many specimen as possible, and only mate with a single one for your entire lifetime, that is entirely your choice." She smirked at the girl. "He won't be allowed the same pleasure." Tay raised a single eyebrow at Ariel, tilting her head. "Ariel, Daughter of Elizabeth, your sexual preferences are your business alone. Why did you call this court?"

"For we seek to live together so that we can raise our children together." The crowd erupted once more.

Tay's nostrils flared and she pinned Ariel with a cold, hard stare. She exchanged a brief look with Eric, whose face was set in a grim look. "Do you have anyone who would stand for you?"

"My mother, if you wish to summon her."

"And mine," interrupted Ben.

Tay looked to Ben and scoffed, "Your mother? And how would you know the wishes of your mother?".

"When I was a boy, still by her side, she'd said she would do anything for me. If I'd had the chance to remain by her side, I have no doubt she would have continued to repeat the sentiment."

The Watcher did not miss the small stab of his words and her lips pursed as she weighed his words.

"Summon them!" She waved and stabbed Eric with a cold look.

He seemed to deflate as he raised his hands. He signaled to a figure at the back of the meeting area. The man was dressed in the olive-green garb of the silent army, long heavy pants that sat low against his narrow hips. His exposed back tattooed with his burdens.

Silence and duty.

The soldier raised his long spear and cawed. From beyond the dune came a silent army. Men who were plucked from their homes at a tender age and raised only to serve under the Watchers, ensuring peace reigned throughout their Quarter.

They marched, muted by the golden sands, and took position behind the assembled crowd. A small party broke away and strode towards the ocean where boats and torches waited. Streams of vessels left the island in every direction as the silent guard set sail to summon the elders and the witnesses from every island of the third quarter.

When the flicker of torch light disappeared beyond the darkening horizon, Tay tutted at the two before her. "This time could have been used more wisely. All of our guests could have been doing what they were meant to do. Silly children with silly ideas, you know nothing of the world."

Ben and Ariel stood silently as she admonished them.

She addressed Ariel and Ben, her overbearing smile parting her lips. "There is nowhere to go, and no way to leave. All the boats are gone. You two will remain here tonight." Looking to the crowd she added, "The rest of you may return to what it is you were doing, but be sure to be here at sunrise, for it is the seventh day, and judgment must be passed." Her lip curled as she finished.

The assembled guests dispersed, melting back into the forest and seas as Ariel and Ben remained still.

With that, Eric turned to leave and the remaining Watchers vanished into the scenery.

Tay growled and snapped her fingers. From beyond the tree line filed in members of the silent army. They wore black loin clothes and black masks that sat like helmets over their heads. Their upper bodies exposed, most wearing the branded A, which was emblazoned across their chests. Ariel's heart leaped as they crept forward, surrounding the couple in a tight human barrier, that reeked of stale sweat and digested fish. The men watched them through their black masks, faceless men who stood silent. Observant. Ariel's body shivered, feeling their eyes on her.

Ben and Ariel sank into the wood. Ben lay on his back, ushering Ariel to join him.

"How can you be so calm?" she hissed at him, wringing her wrist. Her entire face drawn and clenched.

"Because we have done it." He looked to her, a wan smile on his face.

"Done what?"

"We've told everyone what we want."

"But nothing has been decided, no resolutions have been made or passed." Her voice rose in pitch.

"I know."

"So why are you so calm?"

"Because we have stood in front of the world and declared our love."

"And…"

"And is that not like marriage?"

Ariel stopped jittering and looked deep into his face, seeking jest. Instead she found only content.

She leaned down across his chest, the chafed wood harsh against her skin. "You think that our declaration was a marriage?"

"Was it not?" He raised an eyebrow.

She bit her lip, uncertain. "It doesn't mean anything if…"

"But that's just it, Ariel." He brushed her face with his hand. "Is it not wonderful to know that should tomorrow bring the worst, for at least a brief time I could call you my wife?"

Her eyes welled up as she leaned into him, the kiss full of yearning and despair.

"I see you two like to put on a show." Tay's voice sliced through them. "By all means, I can wait."

The two sat up. Ariel grabbed onto Ben's arm.

"Get her up." Two soldiers walked into the circle and reached for Ariel.

"No," she screamed, kicking them off.

"No." Ben rose to his feet, swinging a punch that connected, the sickening sounds of crunching bone bouncing off his fist.

Ariel clawed at the soldiers that dragged her away. The rest closed in on Ben, whose body was already hunched, as a rain of kicks and punches landed on him from above.

She screamed for Ben, his limp body between the confine of muscular calves. At the sight, she began fighting, pulling against the two men who held her wrists.

"Can you put an end to this, please?" Tay sighed.

The balled fist connected with her stomach. Ariel felt as if she had been hit with a brick. Her breath left her as she doubled over, her knees buckling from the force. Falling to the ground, she tried to suck in breath as bile rose in her mouth, the pain like wildfire spreading along her abdomen.

The two guards picked up her crumpled body and dragged her as she swayed like a limp rag doll between them.

They walked off the stage and beyond the dune, Ariel's legs leaving two trails behind her as her head lolled, vomit threatening to erupt.

When her mind cleared she was laying down. The room was white and the fluorescent tube above her too bright. She closed her eyes and tried to regain her senses.

When she opened her eyes again, Tay was standing above her. "Welcome back, Ariel." Her voice abrasive. "I am sorry to have had to rip you from your mate's arms, but checks need to be made."

"What are you talking about?" Her throat hurt and she tried to swallow.

"Accusations have been made. Seems you like to break the rules, but rules are made to be followed. So, we need to validate your mateship, or tomorrow you will be taken."

"What are you talking about? Of course, we have mated." Ariel tried to sit up despite the ache in her belly.

Tay snapped her fingers and four masked guardsmen appeared each taking hold of Ariel's limbs, fingers dipping into her flesh.

"You will be checked." Tay's acid-laden voice hid behind her smirk. "Hold her."

Ariel's arms were pushed down, her shoulders hyperextending, pain shoot down her spine. The other two men pried her legs apart, her hips rising as she tried to pull against them.

"The more you fight, the longer this will take." Tay's sudden airy demeanour sent a cold chill down her spine.

Ariel stilled, her breath laboured.

Deliberately slow, Tay slid Ariel's dress up, exposing her calves, then, baring her knees. Ariel could see the delight in her eyes as the men followed her every move, panting like dogs. Ariel bit her lip as Tay's fingers brushed her thighs, revealing her flushed flesh beyond, and showing off her underwear.

Tay grabbed a pair of scissors, the cold steel pushing against Ariel's skin, as she cut away at the fabric, exposing her to all in the room. She felt the tightening clutches at her skin as starved men fed on her body, nails digging into her flesh as their eyes burned for her.

Tay stepped away to a small white table almost unseen against the bright wall. She reached for gloves, taking slow measured steps, allowing the men to feast on Ariel as she shivered between them.

Tay stepped between her legs and gave her a bright smile even as Ariel's eyes welled, a sob trapped in her throat. "Just relax now, Ariel. This will only take a few minutes."

Closing her eyes, Ariel willed herself to breathe as the latex against her skin induced a whimper.

"Seems like everything is in order after all. Sorry, boys," Tay jested with the men. "Release her."

The hands fell away from her body, leaving behind half-moon marks on her skin. With shaking hands, Ariel covered herself and remained on the bed, not daring to move.

Tay returned to the corner desk, fell into a chair and swiveled, as if she was swaying to silent music. She opened a book Ariel hadn't noticed before and she left a number of markings on the page then spun like a child in the chair facing the group.

"Bring her. She must be missing her mate." Tay winked at the guards who smirked beneath their masks.

"I can walk," Ariel croaked as they reached for her. She flinched from their fingers.

They went to grab her a second time and she retreated into the wall. "I can walk."

The men looked to Tay, who nodded. "Escort her to the stage. You have my permission to use any force necessary to subdue her if she tries anything."

Ariel took a tentative step forward as the men fell around her. She walked among them, her legs straining to hold up her weight as they wobbled beneath her.

When her feet found the wood once more, her strength left her. Falling to her knees, strong arms clasped around her arms and she was dragged to the left corner of the stage, where a new outfit of men awaited her return. Her knees grazed on the wooden floor as splinters shattered her skin. The masked men threw her with a thud and the new arrivals surrounded her.

"Ariel?" Ben called to her between living bars of human skin and bone. "Are you okay?"

"I'm okay, I'm fine," she called to him. "Are you hurt?"

"No."

They fell silent as the soldiers surrounding them sniggered and chuckled.

"Good night," Ben whispered, to her earning a kick in the ribs.

Ariel pulled her knees into her chest, trying to become smaller. She choked down tears and begged for sleep.

21

RESOLUTIONS

They rose with the sun as it stained the black sky with orange and red. The wall of humanity still closed around each of them. The sunrise had brought the breeze, and it swept through the island bringing with it newcomers, who disembarked from boats along the shore.

Ariel peeked through tight muscle and tanned skins, watching the waves bring in the representatives of her quarter of the world.

"Stand." A guard ordered her and she obeyed, her body still heavy with sleep and defeat. "Move."

As one, the men around her marched right, where a raised platform had been set up overnight. Two guards lifted her by the elbows and placed her on the square podium. From her elevated position, she scanned the scene and saw Ben. He, too, had been escorted to a platform set on the opposite side of the stage.

He waved to her. Her eyes darted up to meet his and she gasped at his face, which was once again swollen. His cheek, caked with dried blood, leaked from the broken skin above his eyebrow. His split lip seemed raw and black. Ben held her gaze, his eyes focused, burning, reassuring. He mouthed her name and she nodded, allowing him to hold her from a distance.

The low resounding call of the horn slithered along the island. Ariel shivered, her resolve faltering as the crowd amassed. Flushed faces of newly taken virgins and satisfied men. The grin in familiarity painted on the youth, while the old brought only gloom and melancholy. They had come. The old, the young, the frightened. All assembled together beneath the shadow of the mountain.

The Watchers filtered onto the stage, standing in two lines, flanking the Watcher Tay and the Watcher Eric on each side, as if they had sprouted wings. The women to her left and the men to his right.

Tay raised her hands and a hush fell. The purple-clad council members filtered in. Like a violet river, they meandered around the crowd and settled into the rows of seats carved into the sand.

A silence descended on the makeshift court as the lovers were left to be examined by the wondering crowd.

"State your names for the council," Tay started.

"I am Ariel, Daughter of Elizabeth."

"And I Benjen, son of Catherine."

The council of elders bowed their head as one, greeting the young couple. They returned the gesture.

"Why have you called this gathering today?'

"We want to be known as husband and wife. We want freedom to co-exist and bring our children up together, learning virtues from both of us." Ben spoke for them, his voice booming over the crowd which gasped, faces contorted in surprise and horror.

"Virtues?" Tay scoffed, "Men possess few of those." A murmur went over the crowd at her words.

"Few are better than none." Ben stood up for the men

who stayed placid, remaining silent. "And these few have been instilled in us by our mothers." He let the words hang in the air as Tay glowered at him.

Tay paced like an irate dog. "You know the rules of our lands, and you know why they exist."

"We do." Ben's voice was steady and sure.

"And yet you challenge these rules?"

"Yes."

The Watcher pursed her lips and addressed the crowd. "You have all borne witness to these two abominations. They stand here today before the council, before you in an effort to derail our way of life."

"What?" Ariel cried out, her voice strangled. Ben found her eyes, imploring her to remain silent with a look.

"Who stands for you today?" Tay called out, unperturbed by the interruption.

"I do." Mama Beth stood up. Clad in purple, she strode towards her daughter, leaving the council members behind. If she was agitated or upset, Ariel could not read her steel expression. "Elizabeth, daughter of Irma." Mama Beth stood tall as she met Tay's callous eyes.

"As do I." Another figure stood, she rose from the assembled mass and sliced her way towards Ben's platform.

"Mom!" Ben shouted, his long arms longing to reach out to her. A pair of guards kept her at a distance. Ben clenched his jaw, regaining his composure.

Mama Cath gave him a reassuring look. A fraction of a smile touched her face and she took her place by her son's side. "Catherine, Daughter of Thelma."

"Mama Beth," Tay's voice was laced with acid as she spoke the words, "why do you speak for this traitor?"

"She is my daughter."

Tay nodded. "Mama Cath, why do you speak for these traitors?"

"Benjen is my son." She had an air of pride as she spoke of him.

"Indeed. And what fine work you did raising these children." She didn't bother to hide her distain. "Are there any others who wish to stand here today?"

A murmur rose from the crowd as a single figure pushed himself through. Liam emerged from the crowd and stood between the pair, looking up at Tay.

"I, Liam, son of Ellen, am here to testify."

"In favour?"

"No. Against." Ariel's heart slammed against her chest as he leered at her.

"What say you, Liam?"

"This girl," he flicked Ariel a disgusted look, "played with me since her arrival, yielding her power to torment me."

"That's a lie," Ariel screeched.

"Hush now." Tay raised an arm and silenced her with a cold look. Turning back to Liam, she continued, "How so?"

"She refused my mateship by attacking me, threatening to do it again, and to damage my manhood so completely I would never mate again."

Ariel's mouth fell open as he kept talking. "I got her message, I stayed away. But then she returned to me. She invited my advances, played with me, showed me her body, asked for me to touch her, and then at the last, refused me again, for that pretty boy." He flicked his head towards Ben, his lip curling.

"That's not how it happened," Ariel called again, her face strained and red.

"If you interrupt once more, one of the guards will gag you." Tay's sing-song voice was chilly. She shifted her gaze back to Liam and continued.

"So you were denied?"

"I was interrupted. Given more time, she would have yielded to me."

"Are you certain?"

"Of course. I am just as good a specimen as any other on this island." Liam flicked Ariel a contempt smile. Her jaw was locked, her fists pumping at her sides.

"Indeed. Do you see how this so-called love creates imbalance? It creates confusion and anger. I see this anger led to Ben being punished for his offences."

Liam's face burst open in a smile. "Yes, he has. But what of her?"

"Do not concern yourself with her, for she is in the council's hands. Do you have anything further?"

"I would like to make a request."

"Go on."

"Should it be found that they are abominations and no longer worthy of mating, I would like to take her."

"That is against the rules. Abominations are not to be touched."

"Those are the men. There's never been a woman marked."

"Indeed."

"It will be considered." Tay gave him a pleasant smile that mimicked the smirk on his. He bowed to Tay in thanks and shot his eyes to Ariel, who glared at him, her face a mask of horror and disgust. He blew her a kiss and dissolved back into the crowd.

"Thank you, Liam, son of Ellen." Tay turned her attention to the two women standing before her. "What say you in their favour?"

"You must let them be together." The strength of Mama Beth's conviction took Ariel by surprise. "I have witnessed first-hand their dedication to one another since childhood. They belong together."

"But they threaten our entire way of life."

"They are only children, how can they possibly –" Mama Cath was interrupted by Tay's scalding attack.

"How can they? The old world gave way to urges, lust, desire, hatred. Men and women killed each other for this so-called love."

"But it is in our nature to love." Mama Cath gave Ben a gentle look. "We are creating an entire generation, which cannot possibly understand why they are walking around with a hole so big in their souls, they cannot feel fulfilled."

"Bah, nature." Tay waved her words away as if they were flies. "Nature is vicious and can be changed. We nurture our young and they receive enough love. Then we teach them independence. We send them to the world with the understanding that all of their needs, urges, and desires will be met throughout their life."

"Nurture?" Ben scoffed. "Your rules tore me from my mother's arms when I was still a child. There was no nurturing – "

"You were no longer a babe but a man. You had all your tools, everything needed for survival."

"But I was alone." His large shoulders seemed to curl over his chest as he said the last.

"You were surrounded by others," Tay spat at him.

"I was lonely, and only one person has been able to take that loneliness away." He looked to Ariel, seeking solace in her strained face.

"Do you have anything else to add before we bring this matter to a close?"

"What do you mean to a close?" Ariel screamed. "We have barely begun –" Before she could finish her sentence, a soldier slapped her across the face. silencing her, the sting exploding across her cheek. At the sight, Ben exploded off his platform, surging towards her. Four guardsmen stood in his way, slowing his movements.

Ben pushed the nearest one to the floor and punched a second in the face before being hit hard on the back of the head and subdued. He fell to his knees, his legs crumpling. He clutched the back of his skull, where a light red trickle made its way down the back of his neck, as he gasped for breath.

"Ben!" Ariel leapt from her platform towards him. Strong hands dragged her to the floor and pinned her down. "Ben! Ben?" she called to him.

"I'm okay," he finally replied, his ears ringing.

Ariel sobbed, her face searing.

"See?" Tay begun, apathetic. "We have not even finished the proceedings, and already your so-called love is bringing back the worst in us."

"This is not the worst." Mama Cath's voice was almost a whisper, but it sliced through the crowd, clear and strong, in a way that Ben had never heard. "It is the best in us. For what is love if not life? It is passion, aggression, fear, desire, it is all that makes us human. We are born screaming into the world under pain and duress, we struggle for our first breath as we are wrenched from our mother's womb and into her arms. The first sensation we feel is love."

Mama Cath attempted to reach her son, but her path remained blocked. "They have done nothing if not demonstrated their bond. He will fight for her like we fight for any we care about."

"We cannot take all that we want by force! It will lead to our end again," Tay spat.

"He is not forcing her to stand by his side, nor did she force him to pretend to mate with her for the last year."

"Lies!"

"Love." Mama Cath smiled serenely at the frothing woman.

"Enough of this! It is time to conclude this mockery." The red-clad Watcher turned to the council. "You have witnessed their so-called love, born from lies and deception, fraught with hostility and violence. Should we allow them to violate our society with their poison? Has humanity not endured enough? Must we continue to diminish in our numbers? Must we fade out and let the sea take what's left?"

"There is a reason we have these rules in place. They protect our way of life. They protect our people. They protect us all from these acts of aggression. There is no need for this lust when we have mateship. There is no need to be greedy when there is plenty to go around. And there is no need for violence if there is nothing to fight for."

"But we must fight for those we love, we must fight..." Ben's dispute was silenced by another brutal blow to the head.

"Ben!" Ariel's shriek rang in the makeshift alcove.

Tay remained focused on the council, her seething face as red as her dress. "Rise, rise now if you'd like to see these two punished for their crimes. Rise."

As the women of the council begun to rise, Mama Beth grabbed her child's hand and pulled her close, her breath hot and ragged as she whispered harshly into Ariel's ear. "Despite what you may think, we have always loved you, your father and I, and we have always tried to protect you. This is the last time I will be able to watch for you, and this, my love, is my final gift to you. When I give you the signal you must take Ben and run. Get to the boat. Rosalie is waiting for you. She will take you to safety." She kissed her daughter on the forehead. "Raise your babies with as much love as you have shown one another." Mama Beth squeezed Ariel's shoulder and gave her a tight smile.

She released Ariel and stood up, her figure looming over Ariel's whose body remained hunched on the floor, seeking Ben.

"Rise," Tay repeated and glared at the men's wing which continued to sit defiant behind Eric.

His eyes locked with Elizabeth, sharing a singular tender moment of goodbye.

Mama Beth's voice rose. "You cannot punish them for doing the only thing that is natural."

Tay swiveled and faced Elizabeth. "What do you know of nature? Even wildlife does not couple for a lifetime, and those who do have often been found to stray. After a male wolf impregnates the female, she seeks others to fulfill her other needs, food, protection, or just plain boredom. Our way of life ensures none of that is necessary. Why do you fight so hard to prove that this perfect system is flawed?"

"Because she is my child, and I, too, love her."

"And should she survive today, you may take her home, and that is where she will remain until her dying day, while this pathetic specimen – " she snarled at Ben's broken figure "-will join the silent army."

"Pathetic? You are the one that is pathetic. You are running scared of two teens after living an entire lifetime denying yourself the simplest of feelings."

"Feelings do not equate to survival."

"That is where you are wrong." Mama Beth pulled out her tobacco box.

"Oh?"

"I feel very strongly that if you do not let these two, walk free, off this island, and into my care, one of us will not survive this day." The small metal box popped open as Mama Beth pulled out rolling paper. Expertly, she peppered tobacco into the white lining and rolled the cigarette before tucking it at the corner of her lips, the small metal box clanged shut in her hand.

Tay took in the spectacle, watching Mama Beth's expert fingers create the thin cigarette. Her face curdled. She cleared her throat and began once more. "My dear council, I give you more proof, proof that love leads only to violence and death. This must end now. Our entire way of life hangs in the balance. It hangs in your judgment."

The men remained seated.

"Eric?" Tay looked to him, her voice raising. "Why do you not rise?"

Eric held her gaze momentarily and pushed himself from his seat.

When he spoke, it was not to her. "I am the Watcher Eric, commander of the silent army, watcher of peace, enforcer of law." His frame seemed to expand as he spoke, his smooth voice like a balm to the wounded.

"You are right, Tay. We have been watching a spectacle, and you are the clown." The crowd gasped and Tay's face dropped. He turned back to the council. "Please be seated, we are not done yet."

The members looked to one another as if seeking permission from the other, seeming like fish out of water, uncertainty coloured their features. "Please." Eric swept his arms across his chest and, one by one, they sat like falling rooks on a chessboard.

"Tay, daughter of Audrey, I will not be made to execute your so-called laws. This army of faceless men you have built is your own twisted creation. It reeks of hatred and anger. This masked army is built of the abominations you have created."

Tay's eyes flared as she leveled a glowering look at the man.

Ignoring her, he continued, "Those faithful to me, spears up!"

As one, soldiers lifted their spears, aiming them at their masked brothers. The sound thundered as shrieks rose from the crowd.

"Stop! Drop your weapons at once!" Tay screamed at the soldiers. She turned back to Eric. "What are you doing?"

"What I should have done a long time ago. See, I, too, love

my daughter very much and I will not let you harm her, nor my wife of nineteen years."

Ariel gasped and looked from her mother to Eric.

"Your what?" Tay's eyes bulged indignantly from their sockets.

"These kids." He cocked a head towards Ben and Ariel, ignoring Tay's look of horror. "They are not the first to want more. They are not the only ones to find not just a mate, but a soulmate. We have lived like animals for too long and now we must reclaim our humanity."

"No! It will destroy us."

"You cannot punish everyone because Byron died."

At that, Tay shot him a menacing look. "Don't you dare mention his name."

"Why? Was he not just a mate? One among many?" Eric taunted her.

"Don't – "

"Did you open yourself up to all who came along? Freely and without malice? Without shame? Without choice?"

"I always had a choice. We wield all the power." Tay snarled at him.

"You wield nothing! Not when you force men upon women." His fist sliced through the air.

"Our species must endure. It must survive."

"To what end?"

"Eric?"

"There will be only one resolution and it will be a peaceful one. You will agree to our terms." He turned to the council. "You all will." It was not a threat nor a demand, but the calm demeanour of one who makes easy promises.

"What is your proposal?"

"A division." The word drew a murmur from the crowd.

"A divided earth? Are we not divided enough as it is? We already have our four quarters."

"Whose fault is that?"

She huffed at the accusation. "I only uphold the law. I am not the one who made it."

"When it was made, it may have been necessary, but now it is no longer needed. The population has grown, the water is receding, and new ground has been found."

"What do you propose?"

"Choice." He took a step closer to Tay, who recoiled. "A borderland, one which allows for the co- habituating of men and women, providing only that they be wed and remain faithful."

Tay scoffed at the idea. "And how do you propose that? How would you police the jealousy? The pride? The loyalty?"

"We do not."

"Savagery!"

"Humanity."

Her cold eyes burned as she gave him a scathing look. "And if this human world of yours spills into ours?"

"How can it?"

"You will breed greed and filth within your ranks, you will bring war, and with that our destruction."

"There will be peace. There will be contentment."

"Love is not peaceful. It is pain and agony, it is jealousy and uncertainty, it is heartbreak and hardship. Councilmen and women, you must hear me. We cannot abide this. We must pluck out this cancer before it spreads. You must rise and stand with me. Rise to sustain our way of life. Rise to protect our children and our children's children."

Once more, the council members rose, and this time a number of the men rose slowly from their seats.

Tay faced her audience, a rabid hunger dripped from her lips as she called to her soldiers. "Masked soldiers, defenders of The Watchers, Takers of Virgins and Makers of good men, take up your weapons."

The anxious crows buzzed and hummed. Fear and anxiety leaked into the beach.

"Last chance, Tay, let them walk free," Beth called out to the crazed woman, her tone arctic under the hot morning sun.

"That will never happen! Fools! Love is only for the weak!" Her shrill scream hovered over the swarming, restless mass before her. "Kill them – do it now!"

The frenzied horde, which had assembled to witness events, scattered like straws in a gust of wind, tossed and flung any which way. The wooden floor vibrated with the thunder of feet, and the skies filled with shrill cries and the clanging of metal.

Time seemed to slow. Ariel's eye caught the glint bouncing off the tip of the silver spear as a masked soldier raised it above his head, his eyes locked on to hers. Sweat adorned his upper lip, his bicep flinched as he thrust it toward Ariel.

She heard her mother's voice, like the screech of a forest cockatoo. "No!" it rang out. Elizabeth dove forwards, pushing the soldier. He fell to the ground, where he was spotted by one of Eric's men. His body flailed as the blade was driven through his heart.

Elizabeth turned to the stage, her nose flaring, eyes bold. She bent down and picked up a dropped spear. Then she ran, leaping on to the stage. She grabbed Tay by the hair as she attempted to escape.

"Help me" she howled. Mama Beth wound her hand tighter through the long hair and pulled Tay to her.

"I just want you to know what love really feels like." With all her might, she drove the blade into Tay's body, spilling hot red liquid which spread across her dress, staining the bright red a darker shade.

Elizabeth let go of the woman and fell to her knees, clutching at her side. Hot liquid sapped onto her purple robe, now blackened. The stain spread like flames along Mama Beth's body.

Ariel ran to her mother. "Mama." She cradled her body, planting her forehead into her mother's, listening to her rasping breaths.

"My beautiful baby, you must go now. I have done all that I can to protect you."

"Elizabeth!" It was a strong, deep voice, her father's voice. Her mother's weight suddenly lifted as Eric peeled the dying woman from her. He squared her face and looked into her eyes.

"Mama." Ariel crawled to her. "Mama." Ariel's tears ran hot, landing onto her mother's face, spilling onto Eric's lap.

"Take Ben and go. Everything is waiting. Everything will be okay now." With failing strength, she pushed her daughter away, her eyes turned to Eric.

"Elizabeth. Hold on," he whispered, his voice carried above the shrieks and cries which had erupted around them.

"My love." She grimaced in pain, and he brushed sticky hair from her face. "At least I get to be in your arms in my dying moments."

"Don't say that, not now that we can finally be together."

"I have always been yours."

He nodded, kissing her softly, a low sorrowful growl emanating from deep within him.

"Ariel, you must go now."

She let go of her mother's hand and searched for Ben. He was lying limply on the wooden floor, his body trampled by feet, his head lolling his eyes glazed. She crawled towards him, her movements hampered by a human barricade, some fleeing and others fighting.

From the chaos emerged Mama Cath, her usually calm face drawn and heavy. She found Eric's eyes. He shook his head as she flickered a glance to Beth. Her lips pursed together as she wrapped her hands around Ariel's shoulders hauling the girl away.

"Mama! Ben!" Ariel's shrill screams were swallowed by

the clamour. She fought against Mama Cath, bouncing off sweat-clad bodies and bloodied soldiers. "No... Ben! Mama.!" Her screams fell away as she allowed Mama Cath to drag her failing body. Weaving their way to the beach, the fighting surrounded them, golden sand now saturated with the blood of the dead.

Mama Cath pushed her, urging her on, slipping on blood, tripping on bodies. Ariel scoured the scene around her, the menacing scowls of the soldiers the cowering bodies of women, the violent heaving of the innocent, the curdling screams of the violated clattered along the beach.

She could feel the pain spread in her bones and course through her body. Maybe Tay was right all along. The lawless savagery of men needed to be bound.

Before she could finish the thought, Ariel was ushered to an awaiting boat. Rosalie's familiar face met her, and she fell into her sister's arms, who encircled her in safety and comfort.

The sea was callous and cruel, waves high and dangerous, as if it, too, was feeling the great turmoil within Ariel. With Ishmin falling away, the clang of metal and harrowing screams faded away. Ariel let grief take hold. Trembling against her sister, her raw cries even more violent than the threatening gale as if by the sheer force of her grief her mother's death would be undone, Ben would be in her arms and her father would not be lost to her when he had just been found.

They approached the beach of Inan as the setting sun tarnished the sky with the stain of blood and battle.

"Come on... hurry up." Cath pulled at Ariel, whose body was struggling to stand and walk. Her legs giving out.

Rosalie and Cath threaded Ariel's arms around their shoulders, supporting her weight, then pulled the girl towards the mountain. She could feel the warm sand on her feet and then the soft dirt of the mountain as it stuck to her heels and calves, the soft caress of the leaves and pinch of thorns as they ascended in the darkness. The women halted silently, placing Ariel on the ground. Her body felt heavy, like it could sink right through the mountain and into the sea below, like an anchor cut from its ship. She watched through water-logged eyes as the women pulled away at a curtain of shrubbery, beyond which lay a heavy, almost round rock.

With a grunt Rosalie moved the rock out of the way. A dark cave yawned beneath. She stepped into the cavity, like stepping into a tomb. Feeling in the dark, using the walls as a guide, Rosalie found the hay mattress, allowing her sister to shatter onto it in a heap.

Rosalie kissed her head and whispered, "I have to leave you here now. We have to go. Once we close the door, you can light a fire." She placed a box of matches in her hand. "Just flick, there is kindling and hay just beyond, and a bucket for… other needs."

Ariel nodded through her tears. "They're all dead. It was all for nothing."

"No, darling, it wasn't for nothing. Now get some rest I'll bring food in the morning."

Rosalie made her way to the opening. Cath's a silhouette against the moon light. With a final thrust, the cave plunged into darkness, a sliver of light coming in from a crack in the stone. It sliced the ceiling like a spear.

Ariel's body shivered despite the stifling heat in the cave. She curled herself into a small ball, clutching at her knees. Rocking on the hay, it snapped beneath her weight. Her mind reeled replaying her mother's final words, Ben's lifeless body, and her father's blazing eyes. Her eyes. She whimpered in the dark until sleep took her.

She knew it was morning when she woke, her forehead beaded with sweat the silver spear now a yellow thorn glowing along the ceiling. Her stomach knotted with anguish and hunger, the two playing tag with her tattered body.

She waited.

When Rosalie arrived, the silver spear had returned. She brought with her a basket of food and a clean bucket.

"Do you have any news?" Ariel seized her arm.

"No, my love. I'm sorry, I can't stay. I'll be missed. I'll be back in a few days."

"A few days?" Ariel's body shuddered.

"As soon as it's safe." Without another word, she ran out, closing the stone door behind her.

"Safe?" Ariel whispered in the dark as the stone door fell into place.

A riel woke up. The nausea had returned and the bucket was near full, Rosalie had not been back in days, and if her heaving had not been heard yet, the stench of her accumulated vomit would eventually lead to her discovery.

She counted the black marks she had left on the wall. "Fourteen," she repeated. "Fourteen" she chanted to herself.

Fourteen days without any news of the outside world, no word on Ben or Mama Beth. When Rosalie came, she would barely talk, exchanging her bucket and dropping in a fresh supply of food and wood.

Ariel spent her days looking at the cave walls. She saw Ben's eyes looking back at her, glazed and unresponsive. He couldn't be dead. When she had shed all her tears, she took strength from her mom's sacrifice. Mama Beth had loved her enough to give up her life and so she must be strong for her.

Days and weeks passed, silver spear, yellow thorn, silver spear, yellow thorn.

Rosalie pushed open the door. She silently grabbed the full bucket and replaced it with a clean one, she dropped a basket of food and fresh kindling near Ariel's mattress and made to leave.

Ariel grabbed her wrist and whispered, "What's going on out there?"

Rosalie pried her wrist from her sister's hand and kissed her on the cheek. "The world is changing, there is chaos. Remain here, remain safe."

"I want to help." Ariel stood up, her shoulders peeled back, straightening her spine.

"You've done enough. Don't let her sacrifice be for nothing."

Without another word, Rosalie closed the door, leaving Ariel to sink further into her growing darkness.

The small sliver of light expanded as the moon shone through the growing gap.

Rosalie grabbed the bucket and exchanged the food. Ariel didn't bother getting up.

"You're growing, Ariel. You look amazing."

Ariel nodded silently. "Any word on Mama? Or Ben?"

Rosalie dropped her head. "Mama is gone, honey, you know that. There was never hope for her."

"What about Ben?"

"Still no word."

"When can I come out?"

"Not today, darling." She gave her a wan smile and closed the door behind her.

G rowing a new life within her gave her the companionship she so desperately needed. The first time she had felt the sudden movements from within her belly, she gasped at the foreign sensation.

"Hi baby." Her voice choked with tears as she rubbed her belly. She pictured Ben's hand on the tight skin of her abdomen, his fingers searching for the flutter within her.

"I can't wait to meet you. I bet you will look just like your dad." She ignored the pang in her heart. "And you'll be as fierce as your grandmother."

The nausea had stopped and was replaced by a newfound energy. Love, the fiercest love and desire to protect her unborn child.

She spent her days telling the baby about the island of Inan, her whispers echoing around their chamber. She weaved new tales of the world she had lived in and what it might become when they both emerged into the sunlight once more.

With a voice raw and cracked, she told the baby about Ben and Mama Beth, rubbing her belly as the baby within kicked and grew.

Until she had no more stories to tell.

S he had been hungry for days; Rosalie's absence had stretched longer than usual and her supplies had grown dry. The desire to step outside and eat repressed only by her need to keep her child alive.

Ariel licked her cracked lips cradling her belly which ached for food. The baby kicked hard, reminding her of its need. She held out, she waited, but she could feel her body weakening. Ariel could feel the baby crying within her, shrieking for sustenance. She had to go outside. Rosalie wasn't coming.

She waited.

"Just a little longer, baby." She rocked her swollen body, waiting for nightfall. The kicking ceased, her heartbeat drummed.

The silver spear embedded itself on the ceiling. Ariel stood up, wiping clammy hands on her tattered dress. "We're going." She consoled her baby, trying to find conviction in her words.

Putting out the fire, the cave fell into darkness. Ariel waited, ensuring there were no embers. No flickers of light. She counted ten steps to the door and felt the emptiness in front of her, wondering for a second if emptiness was all that lay ahead of her. Her outstretched hands grazed the rough stone. She pushed against the rock; it stood firm.

She stepped back and took a long breath then pushed again. The door slipped open, easily. Moonlight washed the entrance as a shape released the stone from the other side.

"What are you doing? Get back inside at once." Mama Cath's voice was sharp in the silence.

She slipped into the cave and closed the door behind her, sealing it, entrapping both women within.

Ariel heard the scratch as a match spluttered to life, the single naked flame danced around. Mama Cath's face emerged from the darkness. Mama Cath grabbed a handful of hay and let the small flame travel along the sticks, growing, flickering. She made her way to the extinguished fire pit and released the hay, topping it with kindling. The flames leaped amid the igniting sticks like a child might leap in puddles, splashing and growing, covering every surface it touched.

With the fire lit, Mama Cath passed a basket of food to Ariel, who snatched it from her hand and ripped a chunk of bread with her teeth. The women sat in silence as Ariel scoffed food into her mouth, stopping only to breath.

When Ariel set the basket down, feeling sated, Catherine put her hand over Ariel's. "How are you?" she whispered.

"I'm fine, I think."

Cath nodded. "I have come to check your baby." She gave her a wan smile.

"It's your baby, too." Ariel threw her arms around the woman, who held her tightly.

With the flickering of the flame bouncing off the walls, Catherine measured and examined Ariel, taking careful note of her shape and size, her appetite and blood pressure. The older woman cooed and ogled at the girl as she touched her belly, stroking it lovingly.

"The baby is kicking." Ariel smiled at the older woman. "Want to feel?" Not waiting for an answer, she took Catherine's hand in her own and placed it on her belly, which bounced and jittered under the new flesh.

Catherine's eyes grew in delight as a melancholy smile spread across her face. She pulled her hand away and held it over her heart.

"Are you okay, Mama Cath?"

"Yes, darling, it just reminds me of my own time, when I was carrying my children."

"It's okay to say his name."

Catherine nodded and got up to leave.

"You're going? So soon?"

"I will be missed if I linger."

Ariel nodded. "When can we come out?"

"Soon, I hope."

"What's it like out there?"

"I must go now."

Ariel grabbed the woman's hand. "Please?" Her shirt fell over her shoulder to reveal a gash which had been stitched, the skin still raw beneath.

Catherine sighed, pulling her sleeve up. "It is war."

"Is that how that happened?"

Catherine nodded, not giving her much more.

"Have many died?"

"Some."

"And it's all my fault?" Ariel stepped back.

"Oh, dear girl." Mama Cath pulled the crying woman into an embrace. "It is not your fault. You and Ben, you just brought to the surface what has been lying beneath for years. You have managed to push through the scum and braved what all of us feared."

"Oh, Mama Cath, where is he? Is he alive?"

She kissed her on the forehead and released her. "I don't know. All we know is that he was taken. Since we left Ishmin, we have been getting mixed messages, couriers carrying supplies and mail have been killed along the path. Voyaging is no longer safe."

Ariel nodded, exhaling a long-held breath.

"I must go now. I've already stayed too long. Please stay inside. Please understand we are only trying to keep you safe. They are searching for you. If they catch you… be patient, please."

Mama Cath slipped out, shutting Ariel out once more.

The pain was sharp, like her inside was twisting in on itself. She bolted up in the bed and felt the wetness between her legs, thinking she had lost control of her bladder. She waddled to her bucket and waited for the streaming liquid to stop. It did not. The sharp pain returned as her belly contracted in on itself.

I'm having the baby, Ariel thought, having seen her mother deliver hundreds of children during the course of her nineteen years.

She thought for a moment, considering if she could make it back to the village, if she could make it back home. As if to answer her question, her body broke into another spasm of pain. She knew she wouldn't make it, and she also knew that having her child alone in a cave, isolated and alone, would not be how she brought her child to the world.

Pushing through the pain, she thrust herself against the door, the coarse stone slicing her shoulder. She shoved once more. The door rolled open, and the breeze fell into the cave, filling Ariel's lungs. She stood and sucked in breath through her contractions, the fresh air filling her with hope.

Ariel shuffled back to the cave and dragged out her mattress, hay spilling from within as it snagged on a stone, leaving a trail like breadcrumbs. She let it fall from her hands just beyond the threshold and looked to the full moon. She was smiling back.

Pacing through waves of contractions, she contained the pain until she could contain it no more. Falling on all fours, she howled, her body tearing her from the inside out.

Her screams did not remain unheard, and soon bodies gathered around her, men and women who whispered her name.

Catherine and Rosalie broke through the crowd, bringing with them comfort.

Her forehead was covered in sweat of white pearls in the moonlight. Her voice rang in the night as her body strained and pushed. With the rising of the sun, it spilt from within a precious parcel that wriggled and writhed and cried with a voice so small like a wind sighing across the ocean.

Tears carved Ariel's face as she held her daughter. The baby opened her eyes and Ariel saw Ben in them; she looked so much like him. She kissed the infant, which cried and whimpered, finding comfort along her flesh suckling at her nipple, her breast swollen with the coming milk.

"Elizabeth," she whispered to her daughter. "My beautiful Eli."

Her pain subsided, and Mama Cath examined her once more. Ariel looked around for the first time. The human wall shielding her from the world felt like another womb to be broken, a safe haven for her daughter to breach.

"There are men here." She blinked as her eyes focused on the crowd.

Rosalie smiled at her and her smile was content and full and happy. "Yes. And they have never seen this miracle before."

Ariel nodded as awed faces looked to her and the baby.

"We cannot stay here in the open like this." It was Cath's sharp voice.

Cath ushered four men from the circle, who returned, carrying a stretcher. They lifted Ariel and Elizabeth and descended the mountain. They were followed by a trail of people like a blazing tail of a comet falling to earth.

The morning light painted the island of Inan with its gold and green brushes, yet as they approached her village, the place she had always called home, she noticed the scarring left behind.

The air was heavy with smoke, the blue sky stained with streaks of black plumes which whirled in the light breeze. Houses had been burned and gutted, spilling their guts on the path, standing empty and lifeless. The school, once teaming with song and laughter, stood abandoned, an entire wing blacked and charred. The beach, once beautiful and placid, was littered with wooden and metal barriers as if to keep the outside world out.

The men carried Ariel, winding along the familiar path to her home, which still stood. Solid and strong as the women who had built it. They marched past the creaking red door and deposited her into her bed under Cath's watchful eye.

Ariel was finally home. Her guests excused themselves

and the house quietened. She was at last alone with her newborn. She held her tiny hand and wondered at her speckles of black hair, which topped her crown. Ben's eyes glared at her from her daughter's small face and her small mouth pouted and sucked as if asking to be fed once more.

Ariel attached the infant to her breast and marveled at her creation. She had never known love so deep and so great, and for the first time understood her mother's sacrifice for what it was.

Love is not born of hate. It is born of passion and Ariel knew that if anyone ever threatened her child, there was no line she would not cross to protect her.

In the morning Rosalie came with fresh food and allowed her sister to eat while she delighted in her niece. She allowed Ariel time to bathe and cleanse herself under hot water her stone cave held no such luxuries.

When she was clean and fed, Rosalie wrapped a makeshift sling along her body and placed Elizabeth inside.

"Do you want to go for a walk?"

Ariel nodded, hearing the tentative note in her sister's voice.

Rosalie guided her sister from the house. Ariel scanned the scene through fresh eyes, taking in more devastation.

"What happened here?" Ariel asked as they walked through the half-ruined village, followed by four men who surrounded them, giving them just enough berth.

"There was a war." She gave her sister a wan smile. "Is a war." Seeing the fear on Ariel's face as she clutched her child, she took her hand and squeezed it. "It is coming to an end."

Ariel nodded and waited for Rosalie to continue.

"Mama Beth was prepared for this war long before we knew it was coming. Eric and her, and more than a few others, have wanted this change for years. Our mother had plans and soldiers in place. Men arrived here even as she got on the boat to defend you." Rosalie sliced the sand with her big toe, leaving patterns as she walked. "The night the soldiers arrived, they knocked on everyone's doors, they gathered everyone on the beach and gave us all a choice. Those who wanted change stayed; those who didn't were placed on boats as soon as we returned."

"It was that easy?"

"Of course not. Nothing of this was easy, and of course some decided to fight, taking their last breaths on this very beach." Rosalie stopped walking and turned toward the ocean. "Before she left, Mama Beth told me everything. How she had loved Eric her whole life, how she's wanted more for us." Rosalie nodded as if her mother's voice still whispered in her ear. "She told me about the cave and that it was where you must be sheltered until things would settle."

"And have they?"

"There are still rebels and the occasional attack, but most of the islands of the third quarter have embraced this new way of life."

Ariel nodded. "What does this mean?" The sisters sat along the tree line.

"It means that Ishmin is no more. No more Mating Seasons, no more separation. We are free to co-exist in peace, of sorts."

Ariel took a long breath, inhaling all of her sister's words. "And who speaks for us?"

"Mama Cath and the watcher Eric."

Ariel swallowed hard – "Is he here?"

Rosalie nodded. "And he would love to meet his daughter and his granddaughter if you're willing."

Ariel looked to Rosalie, her heart suddenly in her throat.

Rosalie's face softened. "He is a good man, and he is your father, but more than that, he somehow managed to love Mama for all those years."

They burst into melancholic laughter as Rosalie rose and offered her hand to her sister.

The hospital reeked of sweat and smoke, and the antiseptic smell that often burned off nose hairs vanished. The sisters entered the left wing, which now looked more like a barracks. Cots littered the floor; sleeping men occupied some, piles of clothes others.

"Not all the men have found permanent accommodation. There are new buildings going up every day...." Ariel nodded at the explanation, ignoring the pang in her heart. Ben was a builder.

They approached the door to what Ariel remembered being an examination room, the white door bruised and charred.

Rosalie knocked and a man's deep voice resonated through the wood. "Come."

Rosalie pushed the door open for her sister. "I'll be just outside."

Ariel stepped inside and her eyes fell on Eric. The man looked like he had aged a hundred years.

His kind eyes studied hers. "Hello Ariel."

"Hello." She bit her lip looking around the room. The pair examined one another, each in awe of the other.

Ariel felt her heart as it drummed wildly in her chest. Lost for words, she blurted, "Would you like to meet your granddaughter?"

He clasped his hands and his eyes grew teary. "Would I."

"Meet Elizabeth." She took the sleeping baby from her sling and handed her over to the older man, who gasped at the mention of the name. He looked into her face, cradling the sleeping infant, a single tear sliced his face.

"She was always so proud of you, you know?" Eric looked at his daughter. "And you have turned out just like her."

Ariel's eyes grew bigger at his words.

"I know you often thought she hated you. She used to

lament your fights in her letters, telling me what a strong-headed girl you have become, stubborn and fierce. I assured her it was all of your mother's best qualities and she did well passing them on to you. And although I missed all of your childhood, living it alongside you through your mother's words, I was privileged to see you stand up for yourself. You are just like her." He smiled widely at Ariel as if she was a sweet dream he remembered.

"I never knew…"

"Of course, you didn't. We both did what we had to do to survive."

"I'm sorry."

"For what?"

"For taking her away from you."

He looked at her then, thoughtful and kind, his lips pursed holding his pain at bay. "We said our goodbyes, and had she not done what she did, I would have taken her place."

They stood in silence, the older man swaying with the child in his arms. "We will find him." He looked at his daughter's face, his voice carrying promise.

Ariel nodded, unsure that if she opened her mouth, her pain and guilt would spill out into the room.

"Come here, Eli." Ariel clapped her hands as a delighted Elizabeth took two steps in her direction then fell into the sand. Her gleeful laughter pierced the quietness of the day.

A calm had settled over Inan as the new inhabitants created new homes, as couples lived together and grew families together.

Eric had moved into her mother's old bedroom after Ariel insisted. Rosalie had moved out with her boys and the house became too big, too quiet.

They fell into their own routines. Ariel resumed her job at the nursery while Eric maintained the house, cooked and delighted in his granddaughter. He had never experienced the thrill and challenge of child-rearing and every first was a wonderment, every sleepless night a blessing, every tear shed a joy, and every laughter shared a miracle.

Ariel had come to love her father. The older man regaled her with stories of his love affair with her mother, the secret letters and the harsh payment her mother had to endure in order to secure safe passage for them. She laughed and grimaced at his detail and she got to know the mother she never knew.

"Try again, Eli, so you can show Papa Eric later." She clapped her hands again and waited for Elizabeth to push herself up.

A siren sliced through the quiet day. Elizabeth screamed and shivered at the sound. Ariel reached for her daughter, wiping away tears as her stomach turned. It has been months since anything had arrived from sea.

In the early days of change, she would run to the jetty each time the siren would blow. Mostly, the boats brought fresh supplies, and every so often, more people would arrive. Some scared and broken, most relieved. The new order was spreading, but those who wanted the old ways to remain fought. The irony did not escape Ariel.

"Come on, baby girl." She cooed and threw Elizabeth into the air, making her shriek with glee. Erasing her fear.

She turned at the sound of her name. Rosalie was running towards her, her face flushed. "Ariel," she called out, waving. "Ariel, come quick, it's Ben!"

Ariel's head snapped back. "Ben?"

"Just go. I'll bring Eli."

She looked to her sister, confused. "The hospital."

"Is he okay?" She could feel the air draining from her lungs as she sucked in breath.

"Ariel, just go!"

Ariel sprinted towards the hospital. She burst through the doors and was met by Mama Cath, who stood teary by a door.

"Let me through," Ariel demanded, her eyes wild, her heart drumming in her chest. "I want to see him! Now."

"Of course, you do, dear. Just be gentle with him."

"What do you mean?" She studied her pale face, her quivering lip.

"You'll see." She ushered with her hand towards a door.

Ariel sidestepped Mama Cath and exploded into the room.

The figure lay under a white sheet. Ariel took a deep breath and stepped closer to the bed. The man who lay there resembled the 13-year-old boy she once knew. His face gaunt, his strong body, now reedy and weak. His wild hair shaved from his scalp with only a peppering of black spots on his crown.

She looked at him, and her heart filled with pain and anger. Sitting by the bed, she took his hand. He stirred a little.

"Ben?" she whispered to him. "Ben, can you hear me?"

"I'm hungry. I'm not deaf…"

Ariel punched him on the upper arm.

"Ouch." He winced, not a trace of humour in his voice.

"I'm sorry, I'm so sorry."

"It's alright, Ariel. I'm alright."

"I'm so sorry I left you. I'm so sorry they took you. I thought…" Ariel's face broke into tears. Her anguished relief spilled from her, the heavy stone of worry lifting.

Ben pushed his weak body from the bed, the sheet spilling from his torso. Ariel gasped at the sight, but he reached for her coaxed her chin so that she could look into his eyes. "I'm here now, and we're going to be all right."

"Ben." Her eyes kept falling to his chest, her mouth agape.

"Ben," she repeated, her fingers reaching for the angry scar emblazoned across his abdomen.

He didn't flinch as she traced the thick scar tissue blemishing his chest. The raised A, an angry stain. "Oh, Ben." Her mouth felt dry as she stared at the mark.

He gave her a weak smile. "All they did was put your name on my body. It reminded me every day why I shouldn't stop fighting until I see you again."

"Oh, Ben." She let her hands drop and kissed him softly. When she pulled away, she traced his stark jawline with her hand so that he would look at her once more. "There is something I need to tell you."

His face changed, creases of worry marred his features. "It's okay. You thought I was dead. I don't – ouch! Will you stop doing that?" He rubbed his arm where Ariel had landed another punch.

"Why would you even think that?"

"I'm delirious," he jested, relief clear in his face. "What is it?"

"I have something to tell you, well, more like show you." She smiled at him and got up from her chair. "Wait right here."

"Not like I can go anywhere, anyway." He fell back onto the bed and followed her with his eyes as she exited the room.

When she stepped through the door again, Ariel was carrying a baby girl. She approached the bed, whispering in the baby's ear, and when she was at the bedside, she beamed at Ben.

"Ben, meet your daughter, Elizabeth."

"My daugh – our daughter?" He looked dismayed, his eyes growing bigger, pooling with unshed tears.

She nodded. "Would you like to hold her?"

He bowed his head, unable to speak.

"Go give daddy a big cuddle." Ariel smiled at the baby and

gave her a quick peck on the forehead as she placed her on Ben's chest and into his arms.

"Hi, baby girl," he cooed. "Hi, Elizabeth." He wrapped his hands around the baby, who pawed playfully with his face, pulling his lips and blowing raspberries. "Elizabeth." He exhaled her name, looking to Ariel with wonderment.

"I didn't think you would mind."

"No. It's perfect. She's perfect." He stared into Elizabeth's face in awe, taking in her features, her hair which had thickened and curled just beyond her shoulders, the large eyes – his eyes looking back at him through Ariel's face.

The baby lay her head down and let herself settle into the fall and rise of Ben's chest. Soon her breathing slowed and she lay motionless.

He looked to Ariel, his eyes big with questions and fear. "She'll be fine. You both will. Now sleep while you can. She took her first steps today so you will need your strength chasing after her."

"**E**lizabeth! Come back here right now."

Ariel rubbed her swollen belly and laughed. "I don't think she's coming back."

Ben ran a hand through his mop, which fell wildly across his forehead. "I think you're right." He chuckled.

"Just like her father.'

"Just like her mother." Ben laughed and kissed Ariel.

"You better hurry. If you don't go soon, you won't be able to catch her."

"Speak for yourself fatty," he jested and bent down to her belly. "When you come out, make sure you get your mama to do the chasing." He winked at Ariel and took off limping toward the beach.

Ariel sank back into the chair, soaking up the rays of the

sun, listening to her daughter's squealing as her father growled from somewhere on the beach below. She smiled to herself, knowing that neither she nor her daughters would ever have to don a white dress or chant on beaches. They could always run and love and be wild and free.

T HE END

ACKNOWLEDGMENTS

Thank you to my husband, Clarke that despite everything still stands by me, encourages me, believes in me and drives me to continue and tell stories in the only way I know how.

To my incredible friend Megan Marshall, I love your support and encouragement and how you love this book as much as I do. To Cassy Warren, this story would not be what it is without you and your incredible input. I love that you love my characters as much as me and give them your heart. You are a wonderful friend and partner in crime. Chris Reynolds, thank you for all the feedback and time invested in this book, you've given me so much to be able to create this world and your input and friendship are invaluable to me.

I would love to thank my amazing friend and beta Dawn, her enthusiasm knows no boundaries, her genuine love for books, reading, and helping authors is contagious and humbling. You inspire me to be better with each and every book!

To the amazing Jennifer Demeter, thank you for creating such an incredible cover. Thank you for your patience and enthusiasm in bringing to life Ariel and her world. You've exceeded all my expectations.

My sincere thanks to every one of you who played a part in bringing this dream of mine to life.

ABOUT THE AUTHOR

Want to know more about the author and keep in touch?

You can find her here.

ALSO BY YAEL MAREE

When We Vanish

Coming soon:

Mating Season book 2 – Ben's Story

Why not leave a review and tell Yael how much you loved Mating Season?